SECOND CHANCES

SECOND CHANCES

Stories of Hope, Redemption and Forgiveness

WILLIAM UMANSKY

HIGHERLIFE
DEVELOPMENT SERVICES, INC
Oviedo, Florida

Second Chances: Stories of Hope, Redemption and Forgiveness
by William D. Umansky
The Lawman Press
1945 E. Michigan Street
Orlando, FL 32806
(407) 228-3838
www.thelawman.net

ISBN 13: 978-1-935245-49-0
ISBN 10: 1-935245-49-0

Cover Design: Dragonfly Art & Design

First Edition
11 12 13 14 — 9 8 7 6 5 4 3 2 1

Printed in the United States of America

TABLE OF CONTENTS

INTRODUCTION

Dear Reader,

Do you ever feel handcuffed by your personal failures? Like the things that happened in your past imprison you forever?

We are all entitled to a second chance—an opportunity to get it right before we die, to forgive those who have hurt us in the past, redeeming ourselves presently for what we have done, and hoping for a better tomorrow. That's why I've published this book.

While the stories and characters here are purely fictional, you may come across one or two that strike a chord of familiarity, reminding you of someone in your life. I crafted each of the stories to center around three very important attributes that are necessary for a person's self-evolution: hope, redemption, and forgiveness. It is my sincere hope that you will enjoy reading these short stories and that they will provide you with a spark, a reminder, or an awakening, if you will, to see the second chances in your own life.

Bill Umansky
Orlando, Florida
March 2011

CHAPTER ONE

PERSONAL INJURY

There are no mistakes. The events we bring upon ourselves, no matter how unpleasant, are necessary in order to learn what we need to learn; whatever steps we take, they're necessary to reach places we have chosen to go.

—Richard Bach

As Hurricane Andrew ripped through the outer edge of South Florida, I sat in the women's jail, watching the rain and feeling the wind blow. Back then, the guards would open the big screens on the other side of the bars, allowing the weather to come into the jail's breezeway.

The women's jail was located in the middle of the city, and even though the rain came down in torrents, people still mingled on the streets by the restaurants and clubs. I could see lights twinkling and people laughing, dancing, holding each other, and having a great time.

I used to be one of those people. Not anymore.

I spent a great deal of time negotiating with God in those days. I promised God that if he got me out of that living hell, I would be good. I would be good to my mother and to my family. If God got me out of that stinking place, I would be a decent person. I would stop my bad ways. But God didn't seem to be listening.

Something had gone terribly wrong in my life to land me in jail. I was a former suburban housewife who lived in a beautiful 3,500-square-foot house: four bedrooms with a library, a baby grand piano, and a pool. I had been married fifteen years to the vice president of a national construction company. I worked as an English teacher at a nearby school and used my income to shop. We had a maid. We were members of a country club. We went out to dinner every Saturday night to expensive restaurants. We vacationed once a year to different parts of the country and to islands in the Caribbean.

Now there I was, sitting on the concrete floor of a jail. I had been in that God-forsaken place one week, and no one I called would get me out. Even if I could get out, I had no place to go. No one wanted me.

The truth is, I had become an arrogant, self-righteous, ungrateful bitch. Nothing was ever good enough for me. I was never satisfied. At the same time, I was deeply unhappy with myself. I used to think about that Peggy Lee song, "Is That All There Is?" and think of my life. I had grown up in a lot of dysfunction and had married someone who was stable and steady and dependable—but as the years passed, he became so dependable and so steady that for me he was boring.

I also felt terribly alone. We tried marriage counseling; we read books on relationships; we did everything we knew to make it right, but we had reached an impasse that for whatever reason we could not get through. It wasn't working. It had not been working for several years. But we were a good team, and we were both proud to be the couple that everyone wanted to be around, so we lived a life of "quiet desperation." We started to live separate lives, take separate vacations, and have acquaintances that the other knew nothing about.

My husband began taking a lot of business trips, and when he was out of town, I started going out with my girlfriends, who were also unhappy. We would commiserate over the newest wine or mixed drink, and we would talk and dream of that passion we thought we once had and now lost and thought we still needed in our lives.

One thing I've learned through this is that a lethal attraction can exist between two people. It happens when there is a vulnerable person—which was me—who becomes the prey of another. The attraction is very strong, almost addictive, and when there is a strong physical, sexual attraction, it can be extremely powerful. The chemistry happens almost instantly—it comes out of nowhere, unexpectedly. It is beyond infatuation. You can't get enough of the other person, and the risk of being together is not important—the feeling is so incredible and so intense that you will do anything to keep feeling it. It is very much like a drug. And because it is so lethal, it has the potential to be very, very dangerous.

That is what happened when I met Dave.

Within a few months of having met him, I was living in my own place, and every chance we got, we were together. He was so unlike my husband (who was soon to be my ex-husband). To me, Dave was extremely handsome, extremely exciting, and extremely different. He wasn't like any of my friends' husbands. He didn't drive a Mercedes or a BMW—he had a Mustang and a Harley. He didn't go jogging—he was a bodybuilder. He didn't wear polo shirts—he had two tattoos. He didn't have short hair—he had hair down his back. I thought he was wonderful.

I wanted to share my joy with my friends and family, but when I brought him to meet them, they didn't like him and didn't approve of us. They told me he scared them and that I should be careful. They told me not to trust him. My closest friend at the time said he had the eyes of a shark.

Did I listen? Did I hear? The more they criticized, the more I defended. He told me he was in sales, but I never asked what he sold, and frankly I didn't care. I had money, so it didn't matter. He would tell me that I was beautiful, that I was smart, and that he had never been with a real lady before. No one had ever said those things to me. So I figured my friends and family just didn't know him like I did. They didn't see what I saw. They didn't understand.

And then one day he was gone. I couldn't reach him by phone, so I drove to his place—he wasn't there. For several days I called and called, but he wouldn't call me back. I was frantic.

After three or four days, he called me. He said he was in trouble and needed my help. He said he had run into two men from his past whom he owed money and that they had threatened to hurt him. What should he do?

I remember asking him, "How much money do they want, Dave?"

"Eight hundred dollars," he said.

"Is that all it is going to take to make this go away?"

"Yes."

So I jumped in my car, went to the bank, and got the money. I met him where he said to meet him and gave him the cash. When I handed him the cash, I asked, "Is this enough to let you come back to me?"

He said, "Baby, I've got to go."

And just like that, he was gone—the love of my life was gone.

The next year was an insidious cat-and-mouse game that continued to take my life into more and more mayhem and confusion. Each day spiraled downward, becoming more desperate and dark. I learned that my beloved Dave was a con artist, a career criminal, a drug dealer, and a drug user.

I had been an English teacher. I had never been in trouble. I had never even smoked a cigarette, and I had never been in the company of criminals. I had no idea what I was getting myself into, but I followed him there in that next year, and I knew only one thing: that I loved this man and that he was in trouble. He needed me.

In my efforts to help this man, to save him, to rescue him, I walked into crack houses, stayed in my car while drug deals were going down, helped him through rehab and then relapse, had my car stolen, stayed in horrible places, and got high. And in doing all that, I lost everything I ever had, everyone I ever loved, and almost destroyed myself.

So there I was in jail.

At one point, I got down on my knees and said, "Please God, help me. Help me, and I promise I will change."

Redemption came very slowly.

I had tutored the daughters of a very prominent criminal attorney in town, and somehow his wife—one of my unhappy friends who had gone drinking with me in my past life—found out. Her husband became my attorney *pro bono.* Mr. Lymes was less than thrilled to take my case, but he did it with the utmost professionalism, dignity, and class.

When I finally got out of jail, I went back to where I had lived, and everything I had left there was gone: my clothes, my furniture, my dishes, my computer, everything. My family would not have anything to do with me for months, so I lived in a garage. From there, I got a job as a secretary for a man who owned a trucking business and let me live in the back room of his warehouse.

After six months of living in the warehouse, I went to court and learned that the judge was worried about my health—he said I looked "gray." My mother was in the courtroom that day, and he asked her if she would let me come home and live with her. Reluctantly, she said yes.

My attorney gave me sound advice at the time. He said that Dave was a career criminal and that I should let him bear the brunt of the crime by never being allowed to leave prison—the place where he belonged—while I took on the role of the victim. I didn't follow the attorney's suggestion. I kept my promise to God and resolved to take responsibility for the crimes Dave and I committed together.

This decision cost me dearly. Because I had been arrested several times for felonies, I was unable to get a professional job. I had agreed to pay thousands of dollars in restitution for the crimes I committed and was put on probation for five years, so I had to do right.

The man I worked for in the trucking business let me buy a car from him for $750. It had no paint, but it had ice-cold air. My mother would not allow me to park it near her home, so when I got home from work, sometimes very late at night, I would have to park it blocks away and then walk home. I was not invited to any family functions for years—no Christmas dinners, no Thanksgiving turkeys, no birthday celebrations. I was the family outcast and spent most of those years alone.

I did construction cleaning, laid tile, cleaned fish, worked in a trailer park, and did a lot of waitressing. I worked on the holidays, when everyone else had somewhere else to go. With jobs like these, no one asks you your background. No one cares that you have a college degree or that you once lived in a 3,500-square-foot house with a pool and a maid. Those jobs are all about showing up on time and doing what you are expected to do.

About three years later, I made a decision to leave the area. I still wanted to teach, and I thought my experiences would help me teach high-risk kids who never had much of a chance.

When I applied for a teaching job, I got an interview immediately, but I had to go through a background check. Once the background check came back, I was required to sit through another interview with a panel of county school board members. After this second session, I waited outside in a hallway alone while they pondered their decision. Once the decision was made, I was invited back into the interview room. There, I was told by a school board member that "as God is my witness, and as long as I am alive, I will make sure that you and your kind of scum never teach another day in the state of Florida." I remember getting out of my chair, thanking the school board members, walking to my car, and exploding in tears.

I would never teach school again.

From then on, I built up a shield to protect myself from that kind of attack and pain. I kept doing what I was supposed to do, but that experience stayed in my heart forever. I continued to scrub floors and wait tables, and then one day, a couple of years later, I got a new chance. God showed up.

I was waiting on a doctor and his wife, and he was complaining that his front desk girl could not file anything correctly. I said, "Well, I know how to alphabetize." He and his wife hired me.

From there, I began to work my way up. I went to night school and took classes in different fields of study. I had forgotten that I loved to learn, and I was able to do well.

I always had a terrible fear, though, of being found out. At my jobs, I did the best I could, but I was forever looking over my shoulder, fearing that one day the truth about me would be discovered and that I would be fired and humiliated. I was deeply ashamed of my past. So I had a simple strategy: show up on time, work really hard, do what I was asked to do, don't complain, and hope that my boss would find me a valuable enough employee that he would overlook my past, if he ever found out about it, and let me stay.

This plan worked for the most part, but I was always afraid. I had become good enough and smart enough to talk my way out of any awkward situation, but I never lost that fear of being found out. A pattern began to crop up in this new work life: whenever I felt the truth about my past being discovered in some way, such as being asked to be a notary or if I could be bonded, I would look for another job, find one, give my two-week's notice, and move on to somewhere else until the cycle began again.

Years passed living in this silent fear.

Then one day, I had the chance to interview for a job that I wasn't really qualified to do, but that I could work myself into. It was a job with a very well-known attorney in town named Cab Martin. How did I even get the interview? My present boss was leaving the firm where I worked and thought I might be happy working with this new guy. So I went to the interview, and it lasted three and a half hours. It was the most intense interview I had ever had. We didn't talk so much about my skill level but more about my philosophy of life. We had a meeting of the minds, so to speak.

I set myself up to get through the interview as best I could—I figured it was a test of endurance more than anything, and I thought it went really well. I realized during those three hours, too, that this was exactly what I wanted. I had finally come to a place where I could communicate my ideas about life and about work to someone who seemed to really care what I was saying. I really wanted to work for this guy. He was different, innovative, smart, and an entrepreneur. At times, he was even a bit irreverent about his own profession—which was intriguing to me.

The interview kept going really well, and I thought I had nailed it. When we were finally done, he seemed pleased. I shook his hand warmly and walked toward the door, and then he asked me: "Oh, by the way, if I were to do a background check on you, would I find anything?"

I froze. Suddenly my heart stopped and I could not breathe. He had known all along what a fraud I was. I remember looking at him, feeling the blood rush to my face, and then taking a deep breath and saying, "Yes, you would find something out about me. Thank you again for your time."

I was able to get into my car and drive a few blocks away. Then I stopped the car and cried my heart out. I just sat there and sobbed. All the hurt and all the memories came flooding back. I thought I had done so well in the interview. I thought I had made that man believe I was good, but he knew I wasn't after all. It would never really change. It would always be the same. No one would ever give me a second chance for all the sins I had committed and all the wrong I had done, no matter how hard I tried.

The following day, Mr. Martin offered me a job at his law firm. He gave me a second chance. We never talked about that background check, and I don't know if he ever did one, but Cab Martin hired me. It was the first time in my life that I was found out and honest about my past, and still I got the job.

They say you can't change the past, only overcome it. Mr. Martin will never know what that one moment means to me, and he will never know how grateful I am to him for giving me a chance at an honest life—no more hiding, no more looking over my shoulder, no more fear. I can finally look my past directly in the eye, see it clearly, and not be afraid.

Each New Year's Eve, I hold a private celebration. I light a candle, and I thank God for getting me through another year. It has now been twenty years since that night I sat on the floor of the women's jail, watching people in the streets have a great time and enjoy life. Sometimes after work, I walk out of Cab's beautifully decorated, sophisticated office, and I drive home by way of the streets of my past. Some of the drug houses are still there, but a lot of them are gone. I remember them, and in my memory I still see the people. I can still hear them and see them, but the gift of time has made my memory not as clear as it used to be. This keeps me humble and keeps me grateful—grateful for people like Cab. I have learned there are few persons like him who genuinely take you for what you are, all the good and all the ugly, and are able to see beyond it and give you a second chance.

CHAPTER TWO

FORGIVING DANIEL

You will know that forgiveness has begun when you recall those who hurt you and feel the power to wish them well.

—Lewis B. Smedes

Losing a child is something I would never wish on another woman. There is no comparable pain and no greater feeling of helplessness than knowing I can never have my son back. I'll never play with him again. I'll never see him grow up.

Brett was five years old at the time it happened. I would let him play in the yard, on the sidewalk, and with any other children around. He could always find something amusing to do outside. I never once feared for his safety. We lived in a good neighborhood. I knew the people who lived around us.

I won't ever forget that day. Brett was out playing, and I was inside the house. A group of neighborhood children came to the door. I knew there was something wrong as soon as I opened the door because one of them was crying and sobbing. Another one of them screamed that a stranger had hit Brett with his car and had driven away.

I ran out into the street and found Brett lying facedown, unconscious, in a pool of blood. I called 911. I cried and held him. He didn't move. Oh God, that was the most awful feeling.

In a few hours, I found out my child was dead. A person had recklessly driven through our neighborhood and struck and killed my only son. It was the most horrific day of my life.

A neighbor had caught the license plate of the hit-and-run driver. His name was Daniel Helmsford, and he lived and worked in the area. He had a few warrants out for his arrest for driving while intoxicated. The police found him later that week.

For awhile, I blamed him for the death of my son. I made him the cause of my suffering. I wanted the worst penalty for him. I wanted him to hurt in a way that was as bad as, if not worse than, the way he had hurt me.

A few weeks before Mr. Helmsford pled guilty to manslaughter for killing my son, I spoke on the phone with my mother. My mother had always been the moral paradigm for our family. She had a warm but sensible way of dealing with everyone. Whenever she smiled at you, it was genuine.

I told my mother about my feelings—even my more vindictive feelings about the hit-and-run driver. I told her I wanted him to hurt the way he had hurt me. She listened so well, as always. I asked her if she felt like I was justified in feeling that way, or if she even felt the same way I did.

My mother was always able to explain things in poignant little stories. She told me she read a book one time when she was younger. The book was about a young man who was born a prince, but he gave it up for a life of poverty. The young man did this after seeing how poor people lived. He felt a tremendous amount of empathy for them. He realized that everyone suffers. He realized that if he chose the life of a prince, he would be burdened by his possessions. If he chose the life of poverty, he would worry about living to see the next day. He even realized at one point that he would become bored if he struck the right balance of wealth and comfort.

I asked my mother the point of such a depressing story. She said the young man in the story realized we are all the same. No matter what our role, we all suffer. We all have worries, fears, anxieties, and people and things we love and would hate to lose. Through his journey in life, he experienced a profound, compassionate love for all people because he recognized we are too alike to judge each other so harshly.

I thought about that story. I didn't know how I was like Daniel Helmsford. He didn't know what I was feeling. I still wanted him punished for killing my son. He deserved it.

I went to court on the day the judge handed down Daniel Helmsford's punishment. I had an opportunity to speak, but

I decided not to say anything. He asked the judge if he could say something, though, to everyone and to me. He got up in court and said that he knew nothing he could say would undo what happened, but he had to tell me he was sorry. He became emotional as the words came out. He said not a day went by when he didn't regret having been drunk and driving too fast where children played. He said he knew he was careless and that it was only going to be a short amount of time before his drinking put others in danger. He said he was glad the court had directed him to seek therapy for alcohol abuse in addition to his jail time. He said he'd been drinking and using drugs to escape the pain he felt after his wife died, and he knew he needed help. He said he knew it was not an excuse. He said that every time he thought about the pain he caused me, he would have this horrible feeling, and he wondered if the horrible feeling would ever go away.

When he sat down, I didn't know how to feel. The bailiffs took him out of the courtroom and straight to jail.

Over the next few days, I thought about Mr. Helmsford's apology. I thought about the fact that he had lost his wife. I thought about how emotional he was in the courtroom. I thought about how emotional I was after seeing Brett that day. I thought about how he was going to jail. I did believe his sorrow was genuine. I thought about the story my mother had told me a week or so before. Mr. Helmsford had lost his wife, he had lost control of his life, and now he had lost his freedom. What good would I be doing if I directed my hatred toward a person who didn't have anything at all? I finally made a decision to do something affirmative. I decided I was going to forgive him.

I made an appointment and went to the jail where he was held. I was put in a room where a glass window separated visitors from prisoners. There were little booths with telephones attached. Guards escorted Daniel Helsmford into the room and we both sat down. We picked up the phones and said hello. I told him I didn't want him to be embarrassed but that I had come to see him because I realized we were the same. We both had lost a loved one. We both suffered. I knew, I told him, that he had pretty much nothing in his life now. I told him we could easily be angry with each other and blame each other for our conditions, but I knew that wouldn't do any good. I knew he was sorry, I told him, and I had come today to say I had forgiven him. I told him that I didn't want the hatred to go any further—that it didn't make sense for me to judge him so harshly when we had so much in common.

I don't know if Daniel Helmsford felt any differently about what he did after that day. He left the room only to go back to jail. He pretty much just listened and nodded during our meeting. I didn't aim to humiliate him, but that might have been what he felt. Maybe he didn't think he deserved to be forgiven.

I called my mother and told her what I had done. I asked her if she thought it was crazy to forgive a person who killed your child. My mother, always compassionate and understanding, told me she was proud of me. She said it was I who gained a second chance by forgiving Mr. Helmsford. I asked how that was so.

She told me another story. She said there were once two monks walking through town. They came upon a woman standing in front of a puddle. She didn't want to walk across it because it was a deep puddle. One of the monks proceeded to pick up the woman and carry her across the puddle and put her on the other side. As the two monks continued walking, the second monk became troubled. "We are forbidden from touching women," he said. "Why did you carry that woman across that puddle?"

The first monk turned to him and said, "My friend, it is you who are still carrying the woman."

I realized immediately what my mother meant by this story. If I had not forgiven Daniel Helmsford, I might have spent years of my life living in the past—not grieving in a healthy way, but cultivating a desire for revenge. I would have been "carrying" him all that time, like the monk was still "carrying" the woman in the story.

Yes, I definitely understood, I told her. My mother has since passed, but I will always cherish those little stories when I remember her.

I will never stop thinking about what might have been had my son lived, what his life would have been like, how his personality would have unfolded. But no longer will I go forward thinking that another person's suffering will somehow make mine less. Having forgiven Daniel Helmsford lifted a weight from me. I experience the pain of the loss of a child every day. It isn't any less than it was that first day.

However, I feel like I've earned another chance to move forward with my life. It is a very different life now—and a very sad one, too. But it may have taken this difficult undertaking to show me how to live without the vindictiveness and hatred that burdened me before.

CHAPTER THREE

SINGING A NEW SONG

There are things that we never want to let go of, people we never want to leave behind. But keep in mind that letting go isn't the end of the world; it's the beginning of new life.

—Unknown

The following conversation is a re-dramatization of a recording from a WURS radio show, *Sam in the Evening*, taped on June 9, 2008.

Sam: Hi, everybody. This is Sam, and you're listening to *Sam in the Evening* on WURS. I'm here tonight spinning the classic hits, doing your requests, and listening to your stories of love, hope, heartbreak, and anything else you'd like to tell me or say to any loved ones listening out there. You know me—I'm always open to hearing your story. Let's take a caller—Annette? Are you there?

Annette: Hi, Sam!

Sam: Hi, Annette. How are you tonight?

Annette: I'm really well, thank you. I've been listening to your show for about ten or eleven years, since I finished school and moved here.

Sam: That's quite a while. I know we've gone through some changes since then.

Annette: Oh, I know. It's true. So many things are different now... that's part of the reason I'm calling.

Sam: Yes, please, Annette. Tell me about it.

Annette: Well, when I got out of school, I met this fantastic guy, Scott, and he became the love of my life. We got married after a year of dating and settled down in the city—if you'd call it settling down! (Laughs.)

Sam: (Laughs.)

Annette: We were kind of party animals! Nothing dangerous, but we just had a really good time with one another. We weren't thinking of having children or anything. All we needed was one another. We didn't make a whole lot of money, just enough to keep a house and keep us entertained. We both had modest jobs, but Scott was thinking of applying to a technical college for awhile. We just had a whole lot of possibilities, and we always would stop to smell the roses. He made it easy for me to feel like, "Hey, I'm not waiting for my life to start—this is my life I'm living right now!"

Sam: So you shared a *joie de vivre*?

Annette: Well, I'm not sure I know what that is, but I'm sure we had it! (Laughs.)

Sam: (Laughs.) Joy of life! You shared a joy of life!

Annette: Yes, Sam, that's exactly what we had, and I can definitely look back on the times now and laugh and smile—but…

Sam:… but something happened to your relationship?

Annette: Well, about four years ago, there was an accident. We were driving on a street that we had driven down hundreds of times before. A driver ran a red light at an intersection and hit the driver's side of our car.

Sam: Oh my God. Were you okay?

Annette: Well, Scott was driving. I was perfectly conscious and had only a few scratches on me. But Scott was pinned between the steering wheel and the seat. There was blood on the dashboard, and his torso was twisted. (She pauses, starting to cry.)

Sam: Annette, it's okay. It's okay.

Annette: I know, it's just hard to think about him in that condition, is all. (She takes a deep breath.) Anyway, EMTs showed up on the scene. They had to use the jaws of life to get him out of the car. They put us in an ambulance, and I held Scott's hand all the way to the hospital. He only communicated with me once, in a whisper. Before we got to the hospital, he lost consciousness… and that night I lost the person I thought would be my one and only love forever.

Sam: Oh, Annette, I'm so sorry. That's horrible. How old was he?

Annette: Twenty-eight. We were twenty-five and twenty-eight at the time. Sam, it was awful, but I'm calling tonight because this story has a happy ending. Well, it might have a happy ending.

Sam: Well, how is that?

Annette: Scott and I always used to listen to you, Sam, most nights. He even spoke to you before to request songs—songs for me.

Sam: That's a pretty heavy idea, Annette, that he was very important in your life, crossed my path while you were still together, and now has passed. That's always sad for me to hear when it was a person who had direct contact with me because of the show. I always feel a sense of community with my listeners, and I want you to feel the same way.

Annette: I do, Sam. I love your show, and I think you do an awesome job. That's why I felt comfortable calling you tonight to tell you this.

Sam: Tell old Sam what the happy ending might be, Annette.

Annette: Well, it's been four years since Scott's passing. Obviously it was traumatic, and there were parts that were so difficult for me to stop remembering, or for me to remember in a positive way.

Sam: Yes.

Annette: But I've managed to carry on, even though it hurt inside to get up some days, knowing that I was alone in the world, knowing that I could never have that one special, favorite person back in my life. I want that to be over now, though.

Sam: I want it to be over for you too, Annette.

Annette: Well, Sam, I'm calling because I've met someone new recently.

Sam: Oh?

Annette: We've been going for about two months. His name is Frank, and he's nothing like Scott. Well, I wouldn't want to compare them, but what I mean is that he has just completely changed my perspective on life in so many ways. And he's a good person, he's thoughtful—you know, he's the buying flowers and making special phone calls type of guy. (Chuckles.)

Sam: Well, Annette, that's wonderful! Do you think you are in love?

Annette: Well, Sam, it hasn't been a really long time, but I am kind of falling for him.

Sam: Do you think you are ready to embark on a new adventure with a new companion?

Annette: Sam, I am. Yes, Sam, I am. (Laughs.)

Sam: (Laughs.) "Sam I am"—ha ha!

Annette: (Laughs again.) But Sam, I thought it was important for me to call your show because there is still kind of this conflict inside me. I told Scott I would love him forever, and now he's gone. I met someone and want to fall in love again. I don't want to live in the past anymore...

Sam: . . . but you want to have the feeling that Scott would have said it was okay?

Annette: Yes, I do. I want his blessing.

Sam: Do you think Scott would approve of your new love?

Annette: Well, I think that he and Scott would have been friends in another world. They are different, but both are compassionate and understanding.

Sam: Sure.

Annette: But that's not the important thing, whether they would have been friends or not. I wanted to call tonight to tell you my story and to ask you to play this one song for me that Scott and I used to listen to, to celebrate our relationship. When you play this song, I will think of Scott and the love we had one last time. When the song is over, it will symbolize the end of my grief and the end of living in the past. From this night on, I've decided that I will only look forward to a new life with new adventures and new wonderful experiences. It's time for me to give myself a second chance at it.

Sam: Annette, that's a fantastic idea. What a strong person you've been throughout this difficult process. I want you to know I'm praying for you and I want the best to happen to you in your new life, Annette!

Annette: Thank you, Sam. You are so awesome!

Sam: Don't mention it, Annette. This is my job! I wish you all of the love that you deserve! What song can I play for you, Annette?

Annette: I think it's called "I'll Stand by You"—you know, by The Pretenders?

Sam: I know the one.

Annette: Thank you, Sam. Before you play it, I want you to announce it as the last song that will ever be for Scott and me together. I want it to be our last dedicated song.

Sam: A song from which you might emerge a new woman with new beginnings.

Annette: Yes! You always know just what to say, Sam! I'd give you a kiss if I were there.

Sam: (Music starts to play.) Aww, shucks, Annette! I'm sure all of the listeners out there wish you the best, and I know by talking to you that you deserve to find love, and that you deserve to be happy. Godspeed, Annette!

Annette: Thank you, Sam. Have a great night!

Sam: Good night, Annette, and don't hesitate to call and check in with me!

Annette: I will, Sam! Good night!

Sam: Now, here are The Pretenders with "I'll Stand by You," the last song that will ever be dedicated to Scott and Annette, to commemorate a past romance, but also to symbolize a new beginning for Annette, a wonderful and faithful person.

CHAPTER FOUR

A FIREFIGHTER'S BEST FRIEND

The way you get meaning into your life is to devote yourself to loving others, devote yourself to your community around you, and devote yourself to creating something that gives you purpose and meaning.

—Mitch Albom

Being a firefighter is a dangerous and sometimes thankless job. Some days, a large portion of the job consists of just trying to take up time until a call happens. Calls can be of any magnitude—it might be a toaster that burned part of a person's living room or it might be a full-on fire that threatens to engulf an entire block of houses. A normal day is made up of long hours of boredom and inactivity punctuated by perilous encounters with flames and the scared, frantic, tired victims.

I loved my job for awhile. I felt heroic. I saved people's lives. It was a hands-on job. I was not confined to a cubicle.

But the dangerous part of the job eventually got to me. It wasn't that I became scared of what we did, but that I became aware—very aware—of the potential for danger. If I saw a fire engulfing a building in a certain way, my super-senses would kick in and I would know what we should do. But I would worry about my coworkers, especially the newer guys. I would worry they wouldn't see what I saw when we were on a call. I had one guy lose his leg in a fallout because he went into a room that was weak from having burned. The room caved. It was horrible. Three people living in that complex died that night—one fifty-seven years old, one ten years old, and one five-month-old baby. You don't soon forget things like that.

I'd been injured a few times, too. Nothing really serious—a few blows to the head, some neck and back injuries. You get knocked around every other day. This wasn't any big deal at first. When we're young, we're resilient. But the arm and back pain bothered me like hell after awhile. It started to affect my performance.

And then there was the thankless part of the job. It wasn't that people stopped appreciating me—I know that. But the thank-yous, the grateful hugs from children and parents, the special letters and notes from grateful people . . . they all became fewer and farther between. It felt like an ordinary job without these more personal touches.

I was thinking of quitting. I was getting close to retirement age anyway. Perhaps it was time to do something else.

These were the thoughts I'd been having during a boring week at the station when a call suddenly came in. We slid down the pole, into our clothes, and out the door. When we arrived at 23rd Street, we found that a fire had engulfed the second floor of a duplex.

We started battling the fire. A few guys and I put on our masks and went into the house and up to the second floor. As soon as we got into the living room of one of the areas, a dog ran up and started barking. We kept searching for people. I wanted the dog out of the way, but something told me not to order the guys to take him out yet.

The dog stood by the door and barked to get our attention. I followed the dog, and it led me across the top floor of the building to another living area. It scratched at a door that had a teddy bear hanging on the doorknob. I broke down the door with my ax and found a baby trapped in a toppled playpen. I picked the baby up and met up with the other guys so we could haul ourselves out of the building.

By then, the guys with the hose had the fire under control. We had saved the only child and the dog. The owner of the building, a thirty-year-old in grad school, was still missing. We would soon find out he was killed when part of the building collapsed. The family was immensely grateful when I handed their one-year-old daughter to them.

When the scene settled down, I told everyone the story of the dog leading me to the baby. It was hard to express how uncanny it was. It was also uncanny that my firefighting senses didn't tell me, "Get rid of the dog; it's in the way." I knew, in some way, the dog was there to help us.

As the hour got later, I expected someone to come forward and take the dog, but no one did. It camped out near the truck most of the evening, out of the way but alert. I decided we would take him to the station with us and then try to find any friends or family of the deceased building owner who wanted to take him.

That same week, the mother of the deceased building owner called the station. I got on the phone with her and immediately expressed my condolences for her loss. She was very broken up at first. We got to talking about the dog, though, who had been enjoying himself at the station, playing with the guys all week.

The woman knew the story about the dog leading me to the baby. She pointed out that the dog did not take me to Sean, his owner, which I hadn't thought about before. He didn't take me to Sean, she said, because he knew Sean had already perished. He took me to the child in danger because it was the only other living person in the building.

The woman told me that Sean's dog, Perry, was very smart and well-behaved and would have taken me to Sean if he had been alive. She said the two of them had a very close relationship and that he had owned the dog since graduating college. She said she knew I would have saved Sean if it was possible, and that after Sean's death, the dog had come to me for a reason. She thought that I, or the station, should keep Perry.

I didn't know what to say at first. But I knew that, even if we couldn't keep him at the station, I would love to have a new friend in my life. I offered to take him. It felt like the right thing to do, especially after Sean's mother told me that she wanted me to have him. She was certain I would have saved her son if he was alive when I arrived. Giving Perry to me was like an act of gratitude on her behalf. I was so thankful for this new friend I had gained in my life.

I went back to firefighting with renewed purpose. I'm good at it. The guys at the station are my good friends, and a lot of them look up to me. The parents of the little girl sent me a thank-you note and a basket of food and gifts, and I have a new dog who is always waiting for me and happy to see me when I come home from work. I've decided the meaningful moments outweigh the fatigue, the tiresome routines, and the frustrating people. It isn't about the gifts, the kind words, or the camaraderie, though. I've regained that heroic feeling I used to have when I was younger. I remembered what it is to be a firefighter. It is about working with people and for people.

I still experience physical pain, and sometimes it is a grind of a job. But this is what I do. I am a firefighter. Maybe I'm not a spring chicken anymore, but I have the chance now to pass my knowledge on, to train other practiced and talented firefighters to battle the flames and save innocent people's lives. I am a lucky man.

CHAPTER FIVE

THE PRIEST AND THE DRUG DEALER

Sometimes you've got to believe in someone else's belief in you until your belief kicks in.

—Les Brown

I was one of the hottest drug dealers in the area. When Hollywood stars came through town, they would come directly to me to get some coke, some pot, some Ecstasy, whatever. I won't tell you who I've met. I was huge, and I had my own employees—armed employees—who doubled as debt collectors. There was a time in 1999 when you had a 67% chance of buying coke in the metro area from me or from someone who worked for me.

Those times didn't last.

We got busted in February 2003. We were raided by federal agents. They seized multiple pounds of marijuana and kilos of cocaine from my house and took us away in cuffs. I was dating a woman at the time. I never got to say good-bye to her. There was nothing my lawyers could do. I went to prison.

This all happened when I was twenty-five. I had more cash than someone who works the nine-to-five, happy-horse-shit grind until they're forty. My 10,000-square-foot house was a revolving door for beautiful women who wanted a hit. I could do whatever I felt like doing. I had a Porsche and a Lamborghini.

I went from that lavish lifestyle to wearing an orange jump-suit, going to the bathroom in front of everyone, and getting beaten up on a weekly basis in the federal penitentiary. Just like that, I was stripped of all of my confidence and positive thoughts about myself.

I was never particularly religious. I guess I am Catholic. I started to read the Bible in jail because I knew I wasn't going to excel over some of the more hardened inmates at lifting, fighting, or anything else competitive. When I first came to prison, I thought I had to fight to save face. But after some dental work and stitches on my lip and face, I decided that I could not keep that up. I had to find something else to do—something that would not attract attention. I decided that I'd read the Bible. I suppose if there was another religious text available I might have read that one, but I knew a little bit about Christianity. Maybe I would find some answers in the Bible.

Father Henley was the chaplain at the prison. He was a young man with short brown hair and glasses. He found me reading the Bible one day, and he struck up a conversation. We talked about the Last Supper scene in the New Testament. I wanted to know how much Jesus knew about when and how he was going to die.

Father Henley really knew his stuff about the Bible, and the more questions he answered, the more questions I wanted to ask him. I was a little bit suspicious of him—I'd always been suspicious of organized religion. There was always a catch. But he wanted to talk about the parts of the Bible that I was interested in. He seemed more concerned that I understand God has a plan for me than that I make a decision right now about my faith. He wanted me to know God gave me many gifts and talents. Our discussions of the Bible would sometimes turn into trips to the library, or we would even play a game of cards, chess, or checkers. He came around whenever he was allowed, but we would usually meet on Sunday for mass and discussion afterwards.

I got a job in the cafeteria at the prison. I started to study more, not just the Bible, but also history and biology. I was interested in God's role in those things, if he had any at all. Father Henley was always there to help me and encourage me. I was not so suspicious of him anymore after studying with him for a few months. I could see that when I trusted him, I accomplished things. He told me that he genuinely believed that I could succeed in the real world after a long prison sentence. He told me that even though I would face prejudices from other people, I would be able to show everyone that I was an articulate person who cared about bettering himself.

The week came, after nearly seven years in prison, when I was up for parole. Monday of that week, I talked with Father Henley. I told him that parole meant I could go back into the world with limited freedom, and that would be its own reward. To be honest, I hardly knew how I would get by. I couldn't go back to pushing. For the glamorous lifestyle I once had, all of the pain, war, enmity, and getting mixed up with the law was not worth it. If I did it again, they'd probably put me away for good.

I asked Father Henley, what the hell *should* I do? Go back to school? With what money? He told me that if I had a positive attitude and used the talents that God gave me, then I would be rewarded. I was not entirely happy with that answer, though I knew it was probably the right attitude to have. Near the end of the conversation, he put his hand on my shoulder and said to me very frankly, "If you can't get any work, you can work for my parish rectory. It will at least pay minimum wage, and you have every quality that the job requires. You are absolutely welcome there. Taylor, I want you to know that God loves you, and I love you, and neither of us will ever abandon you."

I didn't let Father Henley see me cry after that conversation. But I did. I'd never had a teacher, father, or any other person like that who cared so much about my success and well-being. I really believed him when he told me he loved me. It was not something I was used to. I wish that Father Henley could have been around earlier in my life.

After six months on the outside, I'd gone to a few job interviews, connected with some old friends, and visited my mother. I hadn't violated my parole. I was borrowing money from friends and didn't always have a place to stay. I found myself thinking a lot about Father Henley. I wasn't sure if he knew that what he'd said to me had struck certain chords. He took on a role for me that I wasn't sure he even knew he filled. I felt a little strange going to him again. He had seen me at such a weak time in my life. I decided I would go, though, and apply for the job he had offered me in prison.

When I showed up at the parish rectory, Father Henley was standing on the steps looking at the sky. I knew he was praying. When he met my gaze, he smiled as if he was very moved, as if he knew that someone had heard his prayers.

We embraced, and I asked him what he had been praying for when I walked up. He said he had been praying for me. He had been praying that God would give me a second chance in whatever way he saw fit. He told me he had prayed for me to find that second chance every day since we met. I knew that he believed that the prayer was answered that day because God had brought us back together. I was overcome with happiness. I had a feeling he truly did understand the role that he had taken in my life and how important his mentorship and guidance was for me.

I'm forty years old now. These days I work in a department store. I wear a tie to work every day. I make a little bit more than minimum wage, plus bonuses and benefits. It hardly ever comes up that I went to prison. It's not necessarily the most exciting job I've ever done, but I'm glad the turbulent part of my life is over. Father Henley helped me move past that. He helped me gain confidence in myself and believe that I was not condemned to be a criminal for good. He not only helped me obtain another chance on the outside, but he allowed me to have someone to look up to, who I respect and who respects me back. That was something I was missing in my life. Perhaps I would have struggled with the absence of that figure for the rest of my life, if not for the person I now consider to be my best friend, Father Henley.

CHAPTER SIX

THE JOURNALS OF JEANNIE

We achieve inner health only through forgiveness—
the forgiveness not only of others but also of ourselves.

—Joshua Loth Liebman

The following are excerpts taken from the journal of Jeannie S., a woman suffering from inoperable cancer.

June 10, 2006

I found out today that I have cancer. The doctor said there is a group of tumors in the bile ducts that connect my liver and small intestine. They are inoperable. She said I may have had them for months or even a year. I only started getting sick with chills two weeks ago. Now I have cancer.

I don't know what I'm going to do. I probably have only four years to live. I'm scheduled to check into the hospital and undergo chemotherapy, but I just don't know. Every time I remember I have this, I just cry and have a hard time stopping. I'm probably going to die. I feel trapped and helpless, like my fate is sealed. I wish that I was just sleeping and this was all a bad dream.

July 20, 2006

Two days ago, I checked into the medical center and was given my own room and bed. I'm connected to a bunch of wires and bags and machines. They've shaved my head. I feel like an ugly, useless creature.

The therapy is painful. I have a hard time eating, and I still get sick every day. Everybody is very kind, but it feels more like pity. Maybe this is all for nothing. It might not even work. I can't believe this is my life now. I suppose no one ever thinks this sort of thing will happen to them.

Writing, I guess, will be my outlet for now, while I'm in the medical center. I don't know how else to get out some of the awful thoughts I have.

September 2, 2006

I've lost a lot of weight. I have a hard time going to the bathroom alone because I have so little energy. I can't keep food down. I thought I would get used to the therapy, but it seems to hurt more and more every time. I cry a lot because I'm frustrated over my inability to do anything for myself. I feel like a burden on the people around me.

Mostly, though, I feel lonely. Dale died so long ago, and Holly and I haven't talked since our falling-out during the holidays four years ago because of her lifestyle. I guess you would call us estranged.

Every time I look out the window and see the sun, the birds, and people laughing and playing, it crushes me because that life isn't for me anymore.

Even if I do recover, I won't ever be loved like when I had my family, and I'll probably never go out to the movies or dancing or any of those things I could do when I was young and healthy. I just get to lie here all day, surrounded by strangers who are trying to keep me alive. I almost wish that if my fate is sealed, my time would just come today.

August 29, 2007

Today the most unbelievable thing happened. When I opened my eyes this morning, I saw two figures in the room. One I recognized as the doctor, and the other was a young woman with short red hair. I thought I didn't know her, but when everything came into focus, I saw that it was Holly! She had come to see me!

She has been living in Oregon with her significant other, and she's been starting her career in business out there. We haven't talked in years. She hugged and kissed me and we started catching up. She told me about her new life and her love interest, about her job, and about where she's been living. We must have talked for about three hours before I had to do my therapy. She told me she would come back, though, because she is staying in the area and will come and visit as often as she can.

Today was such a happy day.

November 10, 2007

Holly wants to be in my life! She told me today that even though she has a career in Oregon, she's going to put it on hold so she can move into our old house for awhile. She has so many opportunities right now, but she told me that I am important to her and that her opportunities can wait until she returns.

I feel exhilarated. I'm so glad I didn't wish my life away before Holly came back. We never sorted out the problems we had with one another, but that doesn't matter anymore. She is here now. I can go to sleep tonight knowing that someone cares about me. Someone cares enough to see me live!

February 8, 2008

I haven't been writing as much lately, but it's not because I'm in pain—it's because I've been having such a good time with Holly! I still have to stay in the medical center, I still don't have any hair, and I have to do things mostly in a wheelchair.

But I don't feel ugly anymore. I'm getting sick fewer times. Holly has been wonderful. She's visiting at least every week, sometimes a few days in a row, and sometimes it feels like we are just having a big, long sleepover. Today she brought me those little chocolate turtles she remembered were my favorite. We watched bad daytime TV together and told stories from when she was little, when she was a teenager, and when her father was alive. Never once did our old problems come up, and sometimes I don't care if they ever do. I'm just glad I get to be with her, and I can't wait until she comes next week!

April 20, 2008

My doctor came in today with a clipboard and told me the therapy has been taking and that the cancer is under control. What excellent news!

She said my positive attitude has helped. I have my daughter to thank for that.

It was a nice day yesterday, so Holly took me out for a ride in the car to go to the park. We had an ice cream cone and sat by the water and watched people walk their little dogs. We talked a bit about why we had our falling-out. I came out of today knowing that we have a better understanding of one another. I know I said some things, in hindsight, that I could have been gentler in saying. Perhaps there are some things we will never see eye to eye on, and we will have to agree to disagree. But Holly said she has forgiven me for my harsh words. That was the most important thing to me. I got to see the sunshine and the birds fly. I was able to be with someone who loves me. I hope I may have many more days like yesterday, and, well, today too, for that matter.

December 15, 2009

My birthday was yesterday. I am sixty-one years old. I didn't think I'd ever see another birthday. And what a birthday it was! Holly got me birthday presents—a blue beret, a straw sunhat, and a red and white bandana. Then she helped me get dressed up in my best going-out clothes, we put makeup on, and she took me to Tony Lina's Italian restaurant, the place that we always used to go on Friday nights when we all lived at the house together. We drank a bottle of wine and gave cheers to our good health. We had spaghetti and meatballs and the house lasagna, and they tasted just how I remember them. She even got the waiter to bring me out a piece of cheesecake with a candle in it, and everyone sang to me.

When I blew out the candle, I almost wished for more days like today, but I decided to wish that Holly becomes successful in her business. I want her to have my wish. Holly made it the best birthday I've had in years. I'm so happy to have a daughter like her. I was alone on my birthday for three years. I almost forgot what it was like to have a party thrown just for me. It was so lovely, and I will never forget today.

March 1, 2010

The past few months have been a roller coaster. The cancer has unexpectedly spread and the chemotherapy has not been having as aggressive an effect as it used to. I am getting sick more often, and I have to have fluids pumped from my stomach occasionally. I am not able to go out with Holly anymore. She still comes, though. I'm so glad to have her next to me during these tough times.

May 1, 2010

I got the news today that my cancer is in advanced stages, and I have at most only a few months more to live. Sometimes it is difficult to keep a conversation going for a long time. I just hurt all over. It hurts to breathe. I feel faint sometimes, and I have a feeling of being called away from the world. Holly comes and holds my hand for awhile every day, but I can hardly do anything fun with her.

I'm not afraid. I'm not afraid even though I know I'm going to die. I somehow feel wiser than the first time I thought my fate was sealed. Today I did a far better thing than I have ever done before, though. I told Holly that no matter what lifestyle she has, no matter whom she chooses to be with, no matter what sorts of choices she makes, I love her. Holly came back to me. She came back to be with me when we weren't even talking. She was really the better woman in our relationship, because she forgave me first. I will always and forever love and accept her. I believe I am truly at peace with her.

June 7, 2010

Today I asked Holly to check me out of the hospital and bring me to the house where our family lived so I can be there when I do pass. We cried a lot today. It was a very sad day. But it was a happy day because I know now that Holly will get to go on. She has so many wonderful possibilities in her life, and she will go into the world knowing that her mother loved her and accepted her. She has a second chance to live with my love, and for a brief moment I had a second chance to live with hers.

July 1, 2010

This will be the last time I write. It is getting too difficult. I get confused sometimes, and it is hard to concentrate. I only want to say a few more things, though, and then I will be able to rest.

I've decided I'm going to give this journal to Holly when the time is right. I hope that she will read it, not to feel the pain that I felt but to know that the last thing I chose to write, the last thought that I wanted to place on paper, was this:

I love you, Holly.

Mom

CHAPTER SEVEN

A PICTURE PAINTS A HISTORY

Adoption is not about finding children for families; it's about finding families for children.

—Joyce Maguire Pavao

I first came to America from Russia when I was eight years old. I was adopted by an American family from a Russian orphanage near St. Petersburg. My biological parents died when I was just a baby. I had lived in the orphanage with about forty other children for as long as I could remember. I had an older sister, but she had been sent to a different place than I had. I had no connection to my real family.

But I will never forget the first time I saw my new family—Dennis, Annette, and their daughter Brenna. They didn't even know me yet, but they were so happy to see me. They hugged me and held my hand all the way home on the plane. I was not afraid to go with them, because my old life was terrible. The orphanage was cold, and we had to eat the same thing every day. The people looking after us were not kind, and there were no toys or birthday parties. Four children, that I can remember, died of pneumonia while I was there.

I was so sad at the orphanage. I felt lost, like no one cared about me. I was a nobody. I had no history. I didn't even have a birth certificate. This American family had rescued me, though, and they gave me the opportunity to be a new person and have a story all my own.

When my new mother and father brought me home, they showed me photo albums that chronicled their lives. They showed me pictures of their marriage, their relatives, celebrations for birthdays and anniversaries, and Brenna growing up. I would look at the pictures very intently and interestedly because they were like prizes. The pictures were things I could hold and look at and think of as having been captured in the moment.

I wished I could have prizes like those because I didn't have any. There were no pictures of me with my biological parents, pictures of me from the orphanage, pictures of me with my sister, pictures of me on my birthdays. I had no photo records from Russia at all. I didn't mind that, though. I was happy to shed my old life. But I wanted to have a history and to be able to tell it from a group of pictures and stories that were about me and that allowed me to hold and remember the special times of my life.

My new challenge was to build new memories—to earn my own prizes.

After I settled into my new home, my parents enrolled me in school. I went to a special class in the afternoon to learn English. My parents bought me the most popular clothes and the prettiest dolls. My new sister, Brenna, who is two years older than I am, quickly accepted me and introduced me to her friends, and they became my friends too.

Dennis and Annette took pictures of me, sometimes when I wasn't looking. I was so excited at the prospect of new gifts or experiences sometimes that I was not even aware of the camera's eye on me, even when they'd tell me to smile. I wonder sometimes if I was even able to make the connection between the snap of the camera and what made the photographs appear.

On my eleventh birthday, my parents gave me a very special gift. It was a photo album—my own photo album! The first picture showed all of us standing in front of our new house in Georgia with a caption that read, "The day we became a whole family." The rest of the pictures showed me playing dolls with Brenna, showing off my new clothes, playing soccer with other kids, my tenth birthday.

I could remember all of these experiences. I could imagine being in those moments again, and I had photographs of them to hold. I was so happy because I felt that I had a history now. I wasn't a nobody. There were people that cared about me. Having a history made me feel like I fit in, like I was a whole person.

Now I'm all grown up and have a daughter of my own. I became a journalist and photographer at a prominent Washington, DC newspaper. I make sure to document my daughter's life as she grows up. Even though she's sometimes exasperated with my picture-taking, I remind her that I was a person without a history for awhile. I want her to know she will look back at all of the photographs someday and appreciate who she is—someone with a history, and my daughter who is beautiful and loved very much. Pictures are like prizes, I tell my daughter—they are things we can hold, and they take us back into the wonderful experiences of our lives. I've started to make my daughter her own photo album, and I will give it to her when the time is right. I want my daughter to have her own prizes and the ability to go to the wonderful times of her life with just a look.

It is important to make good memories and to appreciate the people that care about you. In my life, I was fortunate enough that two warm, loving people took me into their lives with no conditions. I might have been a forgotten child without them. Dennis and Annette might not be my biological parents, but they are my real parents. They are my real parents because they loved me, and because they gave me a second chance to build a real history for myself—a second chance to become someone: a woman, and now a mom.

CHAPTER EIGHT

DEAR MOM

Some mothers are kissing mothers and some are scolding mothers, but it is love just the same, and most mothers kiss and scold together.

—Pearl S. Buck

Dear Mom,

If you find this, you have been rummaging through my stuff again. I think it sucks that you can't respect my personal space. You've meddled in my life for years, and this will be the last time. I've felt this way every time you've gone through my room, criticized my friends, or told me that you don't like how I look, act, or dress. This is my life and those are my choices. I'm glad I don't have to live with you anymore. I just think you should know that you are a shitty mother. I wish you would leave me alone forever. LEAVE MY SHIT ALONE, BITCH.

Jen

This letter sat, folded up, with "Mom" written on the outside, underneath my bed for two and a half years after I went away to college. I left with no particular goals in mind. I just wanted to get out of the house, away from my boring small town, and away from my mom. I wanted space to be myself.

It's not that my mom had done anything to injure me or put me in danger. I was the middle child of three, so I felt like I was being disciplined every time I turned around. That, and Mom was especially protective of us. When my younger brother did something wrong, I was responsible for not having watched him or not having been a better example. When my older sister did something wrong, the blame would always seem to carry over. My older sister, Sofia, was the favorite in my mind—it was like she really couldn't do anything wrong in the eyes of my mom. Sofia was the valedictorian of her high school class and won every beauty pageant she ever entered.

My mom disapproved of my friends and the way I dressed. She caught me with pot in the house, and I repeatedly broke my curfew. It just seemed like we could never get along. We maintained sparse interactions, more negative than positive, and I grew to barely tolerate her presence.

The day I left for college was not a momentous day. I felt a relentless, stagnant exasperation toward my mom that day, just like I felt on any other day.

I thought writing the note would shock my mom. I thought it would give her the message that I was independent and that my mom's interference in my life would stop now that I'd gone to college. So there the letter sat, under my bed at home, as I sat in the quad in front of my dorm, enjoying my new life at college.

A year into my college experience, Sofia was killed in a car crash. An SUV swerved across the highway and collided head-on with the Honda Accord she and her friends were driving. The driver may have been intoxicated, but he, too, was killed on contact. As our friends and acquaintances learned of the tragedy, they called me or my mom, offering their condolences and sympathy. The news had a profound effect on our entire community because my sister was well known for her intelligence, positive spirit, and caring attitude.

At Sofia's funeral, I didn't speak to my mother. Even though we hugged at the beginning of the evening and occasionally became part of the same conversation, the same old silence remained between us. I had my mind made up about my mom—she had overstepped her bounds, so I was punishing her. Sofia's death would not change anything. My mom was *persona non grata* to me. Even after we finished putting Sofia's body to rest in the ground, we did not communicate. We only went through the motions.

A few months passed.

I kept my grades up, and I was meeting all sorts of new and interesting people at college. I had all sorts of classes, from political science to astronomy, and I decided I might major in political science or criminal justice—I was inspired to take on endeavors that might make other people's lives better.

Many of my attitudes and tastes changed as a result of the new social and academic experiences I had that year. My life was exciting and held so many possibilities. I was so engrossed in my new lifestyle that I thought no more of my mother until spring break. Only then did I realize I was running out of the money I had saved from my job at home.

I didn't know what to do. I didn't know how I would pay to keep my car on the road, pay for food, or pay for anything, let alone finance my upcoming semesters. I thought of calling my father, but my father divorced my mother long ago and now was distant and usually unavailable. He had been notoriously late with child support payments in past years. I knew how that phone call would go—he would sound happy to hear from me, make a whole bunch of promises, and then disappear again. He always seemed to like me and my siblings, but he was just not reliable.

I was wrecked by this conflict. Could I call up my mom after saying those things? It felt impossible. But I was running out of choices. With much reluctance, I dialed my mom's number.

My mom was overjoyed to hear from me. She was more than willing to help me out, and I was grateful, but I didn't know quite how to show her that. I wanted to tell her about all of the great experiences I was having, but I was only confident enough to give scant details. This was partly because of guilt and partly because I felt I had to keep up appearances—keep up the appearance that I was exasperated with my mother and didn't really want her in my life.

The next week I called my mother again. We talked about what sort of money would be required for upcoming semesters and how much money I could use to live on while I was at college. I learned that my mother had put some money aside for each of us for a rainy day and that I might be able to get through college with a bit of financial aid. I quietly thanked my mom and told her I would call again the next week.

The next week, we talked about what was happening in our small town. My mom told me about my old friends—some went into the army, some got married, and some were just the same. We even laughed a few times about the antics and escapades that used to go on in town, and we decided at the end of the conversation that we would try to talk every week.

Soon after that, I told her about a man that had entered my life. He was six feet, two inches tall with short blond hair and blue eyes. He played soccer, and he was politically active. He had ambitions of owning his own business. I was so excited, and my mom was excited for me. It made her proud to see me become a conscientious, productive, happy person.

Our weekly conversations continued over the next few months. We eventually got to sounding like we actually got along with each other. But there was still this one area in my mind that wanted to shut my mother out. I still felt like things were so broken between us that we could never really have a "normal" relationship —keeping her at arm's length might be more comfortable.

In late November, my mom invited me to come home for Christmas vacation. It would be the first time in a year and a half that I would be back in my old small town.

I decided to accept the invitation, but after hanging up the phone that night, I thought about that note I had left under my bed back home. I felt like the note embodied feelings I could not take back. And if my mother ever read it, I felt it really could mean nothing would ever be the same between us, no matter how much things had changed.

If the note was still sitting under my bed, I decided I would get rid of it. With it gone, that horrible feeling of guilt for having said those things would go away too, I thought.

On the day I pulled up to the old house in my Toyota Tercel, I jumped out of the car without taking any luggage with me, burst in the door without saying hello, and went straight to my old room. I pulled some binders and stuffed animals out of the way and looked in the place where I'd left the note for my mother to find.

The note was still there.

As soon as I held it up, my mother appeared in the doorway. She came over and hugged and kissed me. She was so happy to see me. But I had the note and wanted to get rid of it before anything else happened.

I tried to quickly leave the room. "Mom, there's just something I have to do really quickly, before we do anything else," I said.

"What's that, baby?"

"Well—," I held up the note. "I said some hurtful things to you in the past, and I'm sorry for saying them. There are a few things I said, though, that would make you think I was a horrible daughter if you ever read them. I'm going to make those words go away." I started down the hallway to throw away the note.

"Jen, I did read that note."

The words penetrated my heart like a spear. I couldn't believe it at first. Then I burst out in tears.

"I was a bad daughter. I'm so sorry, Mom."

"No, baby, you were a teenager," my mom said. "I knew you would say things and not appreciate how they might hurt someone. Look, I know we clashed a lot when you lived at the house, and I know you felt like Sofia was the favorite, which was not true. But none of that ever meant that I didn't love you. I do love you. So much. And I wanted to give you a chance to take back the hurtful things you wrote. I left the note there."

"Oh, Mom. *Can* I take those things back? Can you forgive me?"

"Of course, Jen. I will love you no matter what. You're my daughter, and I would never have it otherwise."

We hugged, and it was at that moment that I realized how wise my mother was. She knew I would want to take back the things I said in the note. I thought about the relationship I had had with my mother two years earlier, about all of the rules my mother had, about all of the punishments I had endured. I realized maybe my mother did have my best interests in mind the whole time. While I changed, my mom stayed the same—she was still looking out for me and still cared about me the same way she did when I was little.

"You will always be my daughter, Jen," my mom said. She took me by the hands. "Whatever was said or done in the past, I love you. I know we might have had a hard time liking one another sometimes, but I want to give our relationship a second chance. Would you do that for your nosy old mother?"

I started to smile, wiping away my tears. "Oh yes, Mom. I really like that idea." I dropped the note from my hands, and it fluttered to the floor outside the doorway.

CHAPTER NINE

PARADISE LOST AND FOUND

Faith is taking the first step even when you don't see the whole staircase.

—Martin Luther King, Jr.

I was eighteen when I first met Elena, and I knew I loved her from the moment we met. I will never forget her delicate, dark features and flowing black hair from the day I first saw her.

We were in college together, and when we first started going out, it was like we were in paradise. We were in a big city, studying new and exciting things, with all new people to learn about and explore. We had our whole lives ahead of us. We had barely even chosen our future career paths. It made me excited to think about going through those life-changing events with this beautiful woman. I will never forget the early days we shared in college.

When we graduated, I got a job in the communications department at a marketing firm, and she went on to law school and became a lawyer. We stayed in the city, and when we had saved up enough money, we decided to have a family. In 2006, we had a little boy, Hunter, and in 2007, we had a little girl, Violet. We were happy and making enough money to live comfortably.

The problem was that we saw each other less and less. Some weeks we only saw each other on the weekends. The absence of one of us in the house would often spark an argument over who was not there for the other person or not being with the children enough. I thought she was too into her career. She thought I wanted too much "me time." Either way, we'd argue about not being in the house, not making enough time to be with one another, and not making time for our family.

We would usually work it out. We both knew we had to work hard to sustain this lifestyle and to send our children to good schools and give them everything they needed. I was hurt she thought I didn't want to be around her, but I secretly thought she was acting unfairly. Every time I turned around, she had something to do for a client or somewhere to be. I guess I was trying to compromise for our own good.

One weekend night, I texted Elena over and over. I expected her home, and I had planned to take the children to a movie. I thought we could all go as a family. I thought she'd be home in the afternoon, as I didn't think a client would take time into the evening on a weekend. But she hadn't come home by 5:00 p.m. She hadn't come home by 6:00 p.m., either. I rented a movie and watched it with the children. She hadn't come home by 8:00 p.m.

Finally, at 10:56 p.m., she walked in the door. I had already put the children to bed and was playing video games. I got up and kissed her when she came in, but I didn't say anything to her about her absence. I didn't want a confrontation. I was just glad she was home.

The next week, on Thursday, I expected her home at 5:00 p.m. I was going to watch Hunter's soccer game, and I thought she would try to catch the end of it. I didn't see her until 11:00 p.m. again. And I didn't say anything. Again, when she came home, I was just glad to see her and glad to be with her.

One Sunday night the following month, she didn't come home at all. I took Hunter to school the next morning. She was relaxing in bed when I came back. When I came in, she came over and started to talk, but I stopped her and demanded to know what was going on.

She admitted she had been having an affair with a client, a guy that worked for a bank she represented. She said it had gotten out of control. Apparently, it had been going on for the last seven months.

I might have forgiven her for that one time, but she admitted it was not the first affair she'd had during our marriage. I couldn't believe what I was hearing.

I learned this guy had taken her to expensive restaurants and jewelry stores. He had taken her to plays, to music events, and had sent her countless romantic love letters. It made me so angry, and I could barely control myself.

I threw her out of the house. I didn't know how I was going to explain this to Hunter and Violet. What would I say?

After several weeks, I cooled down. I decided that it was brash of me to throw Elena out of the house. How could I break up our family over sex and some gifts? She had never cheated on me in college. Everyone knew that we were in love just by looking at us together.

So I called her up with the intention to forgive her and to tell her I really didn't want this to break up our family. Instead, this conversation happened:

"Elena. Hi."

"Hi, Adam."

"Elena, I want you to—"

"Adam, I want a divorce."

"What? Why?"

"Because I don't love you."

I hung up the phone and cried.

We hired lawyers. We went to court. We cited irreconcilable differences. I didn't really care what the reason was. I just didn't want it to happen. I felt so empty inside. I wasn't angry. I just felt nothing.

I was awarded primary custody of our children. I knew that we both would have to have very painful heart-wrenching conversations with them about what was happening. I didn't want to have to tell them these things. I wanted to say that their mommy still loved me somehow.

I moved to a different part of the city. I went back to doing my job at the marketing firm and received excellent reviews. I was doing well enough to buy my children the good toys and take them to exciting places. I would do anything to help them forget what was going on with us. I hated to think they were enduring such unhappy things.

For about eight months, I focused on my children and tried to block Elena out of my mind. I didn't think about what she was doing, but it was lonely at night. I couldn't help thinking I had loved a woman so much and now it was all gone. The happiness I would experience in the future would never be the same as those days in college when we had so many possibilities before us and felt like we lived in paradise.

I started to date other people, cautiously at first, but then more regularly. It was okay. I saw a lot of women. I had a few one-night stands, and I had a few girlfriends. I never really clicked the same way with anyone else, though. It was never the same.

After a year and a half, Elena showed up at my door. She was not scheduled to pick up the children that day. She said that she wanted to talk.

"Adam, I was thinking...I've been very selfish. I couldn't help feeling like I cut myself off from an exciting world when I got married to you. That's why I did those things. I'm sorry. The exciting life is not the same as the life of a person who is *loved.* I was distracted by it, Adam, and I'm so sorry that I forgot that I loved you."

Elena put her hand over her mouth and started to cry. She quickly turned around and walked to her car. Then she drove away. She was already driving away before I could even answer her.

We've been talking since. We've gone out for coffee a few times. She's taking time off work, and we're planning to go on some dates in a few weeks. We're learning about each other all over again.

When we talk about our achievements and the things we have in common, I realize how much I appreciate Elena—what a free-spirited, smart, independent woman she is. We remember the old times, but sparingly, as we both find it emotional to recall our more innocent moments together. I think she knows that I've forgiven her, but we're feeling each other out right now. I think we might be different people than before. We are two different people who have to figure out if they love each other. And it's difficult to start over—there is a twilight zone somewhere between picking up the pieces, reminiscing, and relating to the other person on a new level.

I want Elena and myself to rediscover love, though. I want us to be a family. I want it to happen. I know it's what our children deserve. It's probably what Elena and I deserve, as well. My life with Elena is definitely worth a second chance.

CHAPTER TEN

A NEW BEGINNING: A STORY OF UNCONDITIONAL LOVE

Whatever they grow up to be, they are still our children, and the one most important of all the things we can give to them is unconditional love. Not a love that depends on anything at all except they are our children.

—Rosaleen Dickson

My parents didn't like the clothes I wore, how I did my hair and makeup, or the people I kept around. I suppose it started with typical clashes. They would punish me for staying out late, for smoking or drinking. All they ever cared about was how well I was doing in school and what sort of long-term goals I had for myself. I felt like they weren't letting me be myself.

My mother and I would have swearing matches. My father would come home and occasionally slap me when he found out how I had acted with my mother. He would get more frustrated with me every time. But I didn't stop rebelling. The confrontations just made me angrier at my parents.

When I turned fifteen, I decided I was done living in the house. I packed a bag and just ran away. I made my way out west and made friends with a group of girls who were prostitutes in a West Coast city. We had a lot in common—several of the girls had also run away from home. Three of them had fathers or stepfathers who took advantage of them. We had a lot of things to talk about. Oh, and these girls were fun. They always wanted to party.

I hardly thought of my parents at all when I first started hooking. The money was good, I didn't have to go to school, and I was always with friends. Life was exciting. It was like being able to hang out, all of the time. I didn't have my own apartment, but I was always able to stay with one of the girls. I found that was easier than having a home anyway.

By the time I was seventeen, I had been assaulted at least ten times. I had my arm broken once, and I was robbed five times—twice at gunpoint, once at knifepoint. I had been arrested twice, but I never spent more than a night in jail. It became even scarier to stand out in the street. If it wasn't a thief or a weird john, it was the cops. I had to watch my back.

Two weeks after I turned nineteen, my best friend Dawn was murdered by a john after a dispute about a price. It was terrible. I cried, but my sadness was followed by this hardened, cold feeling. It was almost like I was telling myself that I would have to get used to things like this happening. I was starting to realize the path in life I'd chosen was a dangerous, morbid dead end.

One afternoon I was getting on the subway and caught eyes with a familiar, bearded face. The man was carrying a few bags and had on an Atlanta Braves shirt. It was my Uncle George. He looked so much older now. He said my name questioningly, and we hugged. I hadn't seen him since, I don't know, one of my last birthday parties at the house. He was so happy to see me, and we talked for as long as we could. Eventually, we had to leave, but we exchanged information.

When I asked Uncle George about my parents, he said they missed me terribly and were afraid for me. They hoped that I was still alive and that I was at least doing something that made me happy. It made me want to cry, but I held back.

He took me by the shoulders and told me, "Look, if you love your mom and dad at all, please contact them. Go on their Facebook page, call them, just let them know that you are okay."

He told me that he knew it was my life and these were my choices, but that my parents still loved me and cared about me.

I had to get away from Uncle George quickly because I wanted to cry.

That week I went to an Internet café and logged on. I found pictures of my parents on Facebook—pictures of them in the house, visiting relatives, playing with children and pets, and even with me, doing some of the things that we used to do together. Their life was beautiful. My parents still loved each other, and they looked so happy together. But I knew the pictures without me contained put-on smiles. There were even captions on the pictures that talked about me, about how they loved me and missed me. I broke down and cried. People probably stared, but I didn't even care.

A few days later, I went back to the Internet café and signed up for an e-mail account so I could get onto Facebook. I was able to chat with my mother for the first time in a couple years.

The first thing she said to me was, "Vanessa, we love you. Please come home." I told her my life was awful, that it was dangerous, that I was a prostitute and homeless, and that I missed them so much but felt like I couldn't go back to them. I felt ashamed that I was selling myself to men, and I was so afraid that my dad, particularly, wouldn't welcome me back because he would be so disgusted with me.

She told me that she and my dad loved me no matter what and that they missed me terribly and were worried about me. She told me that she wanted to get me the help I needed and that they both wanted to be part of my life. I told her I just didn't want my life to be like this anymore, so violent and sad. She told me she wanted the violence and sadness in my life to end as well. She said she knew that they had been harsh with me when I was younger, but it was only because they wanted me to turn out all right. She told me it would never escalate to violence again, that she wanted that part of my life to be over for good.

"Please just come home," she messaged to me. "Anything we need to work out, we will. We will always love you no matter what—unconditionally."

I got on a bus and went back home. It was one of the happiest days of my life to walk through that old door in our old house. The house had the same rooms, the same pictures on the walls, the same windows. A few of the flourishes were different—the colors of the walls and the locations of some decorations. The furniture was different.

My father's hair had grayed a little, but he was in good shape as always. My mother looked as young as she always did to me. She was beautiful. They were really my parents, right there with me. We all cried, and for the rest of the night we sat and got to know each other again.

I never looked back at my brief life of being homeless and a prostitute. I have a daughter now, and I always let her know that nobody will ever love her like family. I tell her that her mommy was lost for a while, but that her grandma and grandpa helped her when nobody else cared. I want her to know that I will always forgive her and love her unconditionally. My parents gave me a second chance to have a happy, peaceful life, and for that I am always grateful.

CHAPTER ELEVEN

THANKS, COACH

The best teachers of humanity are
the lives of great men.

—Charles H. Fowler

Dear Coach Ellison,

How the hell are you? I know it's been a really long time since we've talked. I remember we saw each other at Christmastime, maybe two years ago, but I think that's the only time we've seen each other in the last ten years.

I know people don't usually write letters anymore. They usually e-mail and all that electronic stuff, but I didn't really know how else to contact you other than looking up your name in the phone book. This old-fashioned letter will have to do.

The reason I'm writing you is that I wanted you to know a story about me.

When I was five years old, playing baseball was one of my favorite things. I always wanted my father to play with me, and he did when he got a chance. I was just never really good at it, though. I could bat righty and lefty, I could catch a pop fly, I could run pretty fast, but I always got nervous when the chips were down.

Coach, in the five or six years that we knew each other when I was around that age, there are two games that stand out in my mind—when we were playing Beverly Heights, and when we were playing Jefferson City Elementary.

During the Beverly Heights game, I remember you put me up to bat in one of the late innings. There was a man on one base, and I don't remember exactly what the score was, but it was probably close. When I got up to bat, you told me that I had to hustle, and to keep my eye on the ball, of course. So I got up to bat, knocked the dust off my cleats, and spit on the ground.

The pitch came in and sank right in front of me. I swung so hard, I lost my balance and missed the pitch. Everyone laughed, but I heard you say, "Shake it off! Keep your eye on the ball, Michelson!"

The next pitch came in, and I kept my eye on the ball, but I must have jumped at it because I swung with everything I had and missed the ball. Everyone laughed again, but you clapped and kept encouraging me.

I swung at the third pitch and missed again. I struck out, and I know I lost us that game. All the kids slapped me on the helmet when I came back to the dugout, and I was so embarrassed. I felt like I really sucked.

But you didn't single me out. You gave the same speech to everyone at the end of the game about teamwork, perseverance, and swinging level.

The next week, we played Jefferson City. In the last inning, it was tied up at 3-3, and there were two outs. You pointed at me, and you pointed to the plate. All the other kids made noises at me and gave raspberries, but you handed me the helmet, told me to hustle, and to keep my eye on the ball, as always.

I got up to the plate, knocked the dust off my cleats, and spit on the ground. The pitch came in, and I wound up and swung. I whiffed it so hard, I almost fell down! Everyone laughed at me, and some of the kids on the other team started to chant "BATTER!" at me in a loud, annoying, monotone manner.

You still shouted at me to keep my eye on the ball and to focus. The next pitch came in, and I got a piece of it, but it went straight upwards and hit the ground beyond the foul line. Finally, you shouted at me, "Just bunt!" So I waited for the third pitch to come in, and I held the bat in the bunt position. When the ball came, I made sure to make contact with it and make it go fair. It bounced on the ground, but I didn't see it because I made sure to take off running to first base.

The catcher came out and retrieved the ball and tagged the runner coming into home. I had lost us the game again.

The other kids shook their heads at me, but again, you didn't lay any blame on me, and you didn't express any regret at having given me a second chance at bat. I had my head down at the end of that day. But you stopped me and said, "Hey,

Michelson—don't feel bad. There is no shame in any outcome as long as you played the best you could."

Coach, I never ended up being any good at baseball. You never started me again that season after those two games, but for giving me a fair chance I thank you. I played a little baseball in high school, and I played with friends in college, just for fun, nothing that serious. But I went on to have a great time in college and embark on a great career. I'm almost done with medical school now, and I'm going to be a surgeon.

I wanted to write and tell you this story because I remembered what you said at the end of the Jefferson City game. I kept playing baseball even though I wasn't great at it, but I just did my best. When I decided to become a doctor, I knew that it would be expensive and difficult, but I knew that I could rise to the challenge, and I knew that being a doctor would be the best occupation that I could obtain for myself, despite the obstacles through which I would have to persevere.

I can't help but think that your advice inspired me to aim high in my life, I guess is what I'm saying. I know it may sound strange to recap all of these old events. But I appreciate all of your guidance, and your call to perseverance, Coach, and I thought you deserved some recognition.

I was going to call you on the phone and tell you this, but I thought a letter would be something you could hold and look at and remember how you impacted one person's life, probably in a way that you could not have foreseen at the time.

The truth is, Coach, I heard when I came home from vacation that you were in the hospital after having had a stroke. I know that it was severely debilitating, and I know you are at high risk for another stroke. What I don't know is how many kids who played on your teams appreciate you the way I do. It's awful that something bad has to happen to bring people together, so I don't want you to think that that was the reason I'm contacting you today.

Coach, I know it might be crunch time, and these are things I thought you should know before there are no more innings to play. You inspired me, you affected my life, and you influenced me to keep trying no matter what the outcome.

I'm going to come and visit you at the hospital soon. Write me back if you can. I'll talk to you really soon.

Your friend,

Bryce Michelson

P.S. Did you ever figure out who stole your New York Yankees cap that one time on April Fool's Day? I'm pretty sure it was Sam Hoengardener. Maybe I'll bring his goofy ass with me when I come and visit you. Get well soon, Coach!

CHAPTER TWELVE

PILLAR OF THE COMMUNITY

A test of a people is how it behaves toward the old. It is easy to love children. Even tyrants and dictators make a point of being fond of children. But the affection and care for the old, the incurable, the helpless are the true gold mines of a culture.

—Abraham J. Heschel

I became a priest in 2007. I always felt like I became a priest for the right reasons—I wasn't running away from any problems, I didn't need a position of authority because I was insecure, and I didn't have any addictions or afflictions that I thought the priesthood would reform.

On the other hand, I didn't particularly care which denomination I joined. It wasn't the preaching element that called me to the position. What attracted me was the prospect that I could dedicate my daily life to acting on the call to "love thy neighbor." I believe now and have always believed that it is easy to love humanity but to hate one's neighbor. I made it my business to go out and minister to my own "neighbors" who were poor or alone or even just needed a sympathetic ear.

I had volunteered at Setton Palms retirement home and visited some of the residents who received particularly few visitors. One of these residents was Arnold Rossheimer. He was eighty-three years old and a Korean War veteran. An employee of Setton Palms told me Arnold was a famous architect in his younger career. I was intrigued, and I thought I would visit him and see if he needed company or spiritual guidance.

Arnold Rossheimer's room was number 306, on the third floor of Setton Palms. When I first visited him, he asked the attendant if they brought me in because he was about to die. She looked exasperated with him and told him that I was just here to visit. Rossheimer laughed heartily at his own dark joke about his mortality. He welcomed me into his room and told me to sit down.

I told him that I had heard about his being a famous architect. He made a face, but then he opened up about it. He told me he loved designing and building buildings, but he thought his life's work went unappreciated. He told me he excelled in school and went on to design for big businesses.

He asked if I'd ever been to the local library. I told him that I had gone by it a few times but was very well aware of the façade of the building. He told me he had designed that building, as well as the annex building and the atriums of two surrounding buildings. I was very familiar with that area of town. He said he had also designed the Stetson Bank building downtown and the Heimholz business complex on 61st Street. I told him, that I thought it was excellent work and that people used and appreciated those places every single day.

He shrugged. He said maybe people appreciated them at one time, but the city was dominated by new structures and artwork and was not as clean or as well kept as it used to be. He felt that people did not appreciate the older and more essential characteristics of the city, and he identified with that sentiment in his architecture. We talked for about an hour that day about ideals, beauty, value—things I remember talking about in college art classes. All the while, I had the idea that he had to tone down some of the subject matter so I could keep up with him. Never once did I get the idea that this man was unstable or experiencing symptoms of dementia.

I soon found that I was talking to a very deep person with a vast knowledge of science, physics, and spirituality. I asked him if he minded if I came back the next week, and he shrugged, gave a half smile, and told me I could. I thought he appreciated my company, and I found him fascinating.

The next week, when I came back, he started to tell me about the war, about how he had been lost for fifty-one days in central North Korea. He and two other soldiers were separated from their platoon after an attack, and they were operating as an outfit until they met contacts. He was the only one of the three men to survive the experience of getting lost behind enemy lines.

He said he'd watched one of his friends get shot at point-blank range during the experience. It was a horrible, ghastly experience for him, but he never talked about it in an agitated manner, as if life had promised him something better or more glamorous. He put on a solemn face and eyes when he talked about the two other soldiers, because they were his friends. But he remained composed and optimistic in his storytelling.

I learned he finally met up with a platoon who had him flown out, and he was able to go home. He had only broken his nose and lost his left middle finger, he said in an almost relieved manner. He directed me to open his dresser drawer, and inside was his Purple Heart.

Rossheimer said his army experience was not something he regretted. He said he thought if he had stayed and remained an architect during the time of the war, maybe he could have remained relevant or had more influence on how our city appeared. I told him what faith says about using one's talents, and he smiled and thanked me for the kind words, but I could tell he took the words with a grain of salt.

When I went home that night, I wrote a bit about Rossheimer's experiences and said a prayer for him.

When I returned the next week, I entered the room and Rossheimer was standing looking out the window. I gave a greeting to him, but he did not turn around. I went over and put my hand on his shoulder. He looked at me and asked, with his half smile, "Who are you?"

I said to him, "Well, I'm Father Dean Clemens. We talk sometimes, don't you know me?"

He replied, "No, but you're welcome to stay. I don't have many visitors these days."

I felt awful because he might have been serious. He might have really forgotten who I was. We went on talking to each other about architecture, people, the world. I went on getting to know him. I bid him goodnight as friends do to one another when we left, and I had the parting impression that he eventually remembered who I was.

The attendant caught me on the way out and told me that a doctor had recently diagnosed Rossheimer as entering early stages of dementia. It broke my heart to see such an accomplished person have to suffer from such an affliction. I figured the least I could do was keep going and visiting him.

That's what I did every week. Sometimes more than once, I went and heard a story or had a debate with Arnold Rossheimer. Sometimes he knew who I was, and sometimes he didn't. It seemed there was a period of his life where everything was clear, and then suddenly a cut-off point where his experience became cloudy. He became frustrated with it only once in awhile, and only once did he become so angry that he lashed out.

It hurt me to see him like that—his mind deteriorating—but I stayed with him and was his friend, even when he didn't know me. Attendants told me that it was in fact true that he had few other visitors. Most of his family had passed on, and he had only one son who was killed in an accident. Rossheimer was a genius in his time, but I could tell he felt outshone, washed-up, and forgotten by the people who once appreciated him.

In October of that year, after I had been going to see him for two months, Arnold Rossheimer died in his sleep of natural causes. I suppose God just called him at that moment.

I got the phone call the next afternoon. I wept on the spot, even though some of the other people at the rectory were around. I wasn't ashamed to cry over the death of such a great man. I cried again after reading his obituary in the newspaper, along with the advertisement of his funeral.

The day of the funeral, the parking lots and surrounding areas were packed. People were crowded outside the church. The church was packed with people who were his friends from different places, positive acquaintances he had made, and distant relatives who had heard the word of his passing. I prepared to say the mass for him, and to give my own eulogy.

The first thing I did was say thank you to everyone, on the part of Arnold Rossheimer, for I secretly feared that his life of rich accomplishments and bravery would go unnoticed. I told them that Arnold Rossheimer would have been so happy to know that people from far and wide appreciated his work and his artistic values. I said to everyone that I had become his personal friend during the end of his life when his mind and sometimes his nerves were becoming frayed by a long, sometimes arduous life. I told everyone that Arnold Rossheimer was a genius and a person who changed our city for the best and that it was a fantastic and blessed thing that we could all be together to celebrate his life.

Everyone applauded at the end of my eulogy. The crowd followed the casket out the door and showed up again at the cemetery. There must have been a thousand people. Everyone was quiet and polite during the service but prone to erupt into spontaneous cheers and applause after mentions of his name. What a scene it was! This was the first funeral I had ever been to, or given, for that matter, that seemed like a celebration of someone's life, rather than everyone suffering openly at the loss of a loved one.

Arnold Rossheimer was truly a genius and a hero. He had an intense spirituality and love of life, despite the suffering he went through, and despite the loneliness he was feeling at the end of his life. I was so happy to have been able to be part of his life, if for only a brief period. I started out visiting Rossheimer for my own reasons, but I ended up taking up for him.

I suppose that is what we are supposed to learn from the "love thy neighbor" commandment—that there is something valuable in everyone, something worth establishing, something worth celebrating. In his life, I did my best to support Arnold

Rossheimer when he felt he had been forgotten. I would like to believe that I helped re-establish Rossheimer as a great person—a person who had influence on the world around him. In his death, I would like to believe that I celebrated Rossheimer the way he ought to have been celebrated—as a courageous, talented, charming, kindhearted child of God.

CHAPTER THIRTEEN

REBIRTH

Although the world is full of suffering, it
is also full of the overcoming of it.

—Helen Keller

I'm Roger Brooks, and I'm fifty years old, since last Tuesday. I used to be a fighter in mixed martial arts competitions. I have a black belt in jujitsu, and I am an expert in capoeira and extension fighting.

Unfortunately, I am not able to fight competitively again, but I am thankful to be still alive. Before my accident, I didn't know what I believed. I wasn't sure if I was atheist or agnostic, or if I believed in God or something else. After my accident, I gained a more significant understanding of what it means to live and where to find true purpose in life.

I was kind of an excitement junkie. Bungee jumping, skydiving—you name it, that was my game. I loved to ride my

Harley motorcycle down the long straightaways in Orlando—that was one of my favorite things.

One night, I was riding down Highway 50, and a taxicab came just a little bit too far into the intersection. I collided with the side of it at about 40 mph. I was propelled into the air like a rag doll, hit the top of my head on the hood of the taxicab, and fell directly on my lower spine. I found out later that witnesses who saw the accident said they were certain I was dead after it happened. Thankfully, I wasn't dead. However, I was nearly completely paralyzed in my back and parts of my arms and legs. Doctors said I would never be able to walk again, let alone fight in competitions.

People say they have experiences during traumatic events like this. I've heard of people having out-of-body experiences, or meeting lost loved ones, or seeing a bright, vibrant light. I didn't have any of these experiences. When I woke up in the hospital and the confusion settled in, I was not inspired or spiritually enlightened. I was angry. I felt useless. It was as if I had even less meaning in my life than before, and I was not certain where to even find meaning.

All I could do was say to myself, *Oh no, oh no... I can't reverse what just happened.* I knew that my body, which I had worked so hard to maintain, was bent up and broken by blows worse than those inflicted by the most skilled fighters.

That night, when my wife, Kelly, appeared in my hospital room, I was not even sure how long she was there before I could acknowledge and converse with her. I was unable to talk, even after I was conscious. I wanted her to know I was all right and that I loved her, but secretly I was profoundly unhappy and wondered if I would be a burden on everyone around me for the rest of my life.

I asked myself why the doctors even tried to save me if they knew I would be so useless. I felt that my life would be worthless and that continuing to live might just make me dislike myself more and more. I couldn't be me—I couldn't fight, and I for sure couldn't ride a motorcycle anymore. The accident was almost like the opposite of a spiritual event for me—it made me have less faith.

I met with a physical rehabilitation physician at the direction of my doctor. The therapist's name was Henry Moore. Dr. Moore was very no-nonsense. I wasn't sure what he believed about God, but he, unlike other doctors who evaluated my condition, told me that I could walk again.

I asked him what had to happen, and he told me three things. First, he said I had to exercise. Second, he said I had to be willing to endure more pain. And third, he said I had to want to live. The first and second points were fine with me—exercise and enduring pain were already easy for me to do—but I asked him why he added that I had to want to live.

He responded that the body did not—could not—heal without the will to live. He said that if I didn't want to live, I could be like this for my whole life.

This was difficult for me because I had so little hope that I could be the same person I was before. I had a hard time wanting to live.

I wasn't sure if Dr. Moore knew this was a challenge for me. The therapy was grueling. Sometimes I would make little or no progress in a day. I would become frustrated because I knew what I wanted my limbs to do, but they would not cooperate. It made me so angry. I had taken so many things for granted about my body. But now I couldn't move my fingers, let alone throw a good jab or strike. I couldn't hug Kelly when she hugged me. My daily routines were embarrassing and humiliating. I was a 280-pound man who had to have someone brush his teeth, clean him, and help him use the bathroom.

As the days passed, I began to cry openly, sometimes more than once a day. I could not keep my pride on my face. Every normal activity was a struggle, and it was hard to want to go on. Even though Kelly was there for me, I felt like it hurt her to see me so debilitated and frustrated. I would have bad thoughts often—thoughts about being a burden and how everyone might be better off without me being around. I was a broken person.

About forty-five days after the accident, I received a phone call that changed everything. It was Kelly, and she told me we were going to have a baby. I was going to be a father. I was shocked, and then I was overcome with tremendous joy. We both cried, but I couldn't even say a single sentence through the phone without sobbing, and Kelly finally asked me what was wrong.

I confessed to Kelly that I had been thinking of ending my life if the opportunity arose because I had no reason to want to live. If I couldn't fight or ride my motorcycle or skydive or be intimate with her—if I couldn't do all the things my body allowed me to do before the accident, my life had no quality to it, and I was just going to throw it away. But now, I would have new goals. I would show our child the world, teach him or her to ride a bicycle, play an instrument, and live harmoniously with others. It made me so happy, and it seemed to lift the burden of emptiness and futility that I had allowed to grow in my mind. I felt so rejuvenated, like a new type of faith had sprung up within me.

I continued going to physical therapy. Every day, I thought to myself that learning to move my limbs again would help me teach my son or daughter how to do things too, and that inspired me. I wondered what interests my child would have, and I looked forward to helping him or her achieve goals and be happy. All of this gave me confidence and the will to live that Dr. Moore said was vital to my recovery.

Gradually, I was able to show small triumphs in moving my feet or my right hand. After a few months, I could move both of my feet a little and most of the fingers on my right hand. At the end of three months, I could work a wheelchair for myself, and I could shower, shave, and brush my teeth. By the end of nine months, I could move my legs and do most daily tasks on my own, but I still had to use a wheelchair. I was able to be there when my son was born, and it was one of the happiest moments of my life.

I never did ride a motorcycle again. But the birth of my son opened up a new collection of goals that were far greater than thrill-seeking. I taught him about the world, how to ride a bicycle, and how to live with others. Being with my son also encouraged me to be more active in other areas in my life, and today I run a martial arts school. I am rarely able to get out on the floor to practice forms or to spar with the students, but my son is eleven years old now, he is a brown belt in jujitsu, and he is on the floor every day.

I am so proud of him.

I will never forget that my son gave me a second chance at life and that I almost chose not to be here and be his father. I'm still not certain of whether I am a spiritual or religious person, but I do believe something or someone out there presented me with a shining opportunity to regain my will to live, to heal, and to rise to the responsibility of being a father. I'm not sorry that my accident happened. I'm not sorry that I endured so much pain. I would not wish the accident away. If I never had had my accident, my faith never would have changed, and I may have taken the same things for granted that I always had. I know in my heart that if things hadn't happened this way, I would never have gained a higher understanding of what it means to live and where to find such purpose in my life.

CHAPTER FOURTEEN

CYBERBULLIES: HOW THEY WRECKED AND SAVED A LIFE

I think the hardest part about being a teenager is dealing with other teenagers—the criticism and the ridicule, the gossip and the rumors.

—Beverly Mitchell

September 24, 9:02 pm—RadicalLife9: You are a fat slut.

October 1, 5:44 pm—ChamomileT000: You should eat sh*t and die. Ha!

November 4, 4:35 pm—BlackHairedQT: Jeremy doesn't like you. None of the boys like you.

January 2, 6:07 pm—TheEnforcers26555: F*ck you, you ho.

March 6, 7:23 pm—TMNT9334: You are an ugly bitch with no friends and no one will ever love you.

These were just a few texts and instant messages that people sent me. They sent them to me at all times of the day and littered my Myspace page with similar comments. It seemed like it would never stop. The people who made fun of me in high school were the same people who made fun of me in elementary school. They mocked me for the way I looked, the way I dressed, my opinions, which music I listened to, which boys I might have liked. The girls were especially mean to me. They texted me in school with something nasty like, "You can't ever have that boy," or "That was a stupid thing to say," whenever they saw me do something they thought they had to make fun of. I cried. I had maybe two people I'd call friends, but one was a boy and the other one distanced herself from me in school.

I did my best to blend in. I tried to be friendly to people. I tried to be pretty. It seemed like the more I tried to be a better person, the more everyone else hated me. I started to think that maybe I did have a weight problem, maybe I would always be unattractive to boys, maybe I was a loser. It was true that I never had a boyfriend. Maybe I was too ugly to be loved.

That's what the texts told me.

In the evenings, and even on weekends, I sat alone in my room in the house, with only the television and the computer as companions. Sure, I had friends online from other places, but it wasn't the same. They know the people did that were making fun of me. They told me that I had to ignore them or just be myself. I got tired of this advice.

One Friday night, I was talking to a few people online and doing my homework at the same time. Three girls started messaging me and telling me that I sucked because I was not out at the dance that was going on at the community center. They started to tell me who was going to be there and that all of the boys there would think I was ugly anyway and wouldn't want to dance with me. They called me an ugly pig and said I should die.

I cried as I typed back. I told them they would be sorry for saying these things.

Then I just lost it. I typed a goodbye letter and printed it out. I put on some makeup. I left the house in a hurry without disturbing my parents.

I only had a vague idea of where I was going. It was almost like I acted on the first idea that came into my head when I left the house. I came to a bridge above an overpass. I rode by that area nearly every day. I folded up the goodbye letter and put it in my jeans pocket. I stood up on the barrier. I looked at the horizon and down at the cars passing underneath. I played with the charm I wore around my neck, a gift from my mother on my eleventh birthday. I cried and thought about how I wouldn't have any more experiences like receiving a pretty piece of jewelry. Then I thought I wouldn't have them anyway, because if I lived no one would love me. At least this way, I wouldn't know what I was missing.

I took a deep breath. I leaned over and let myself fall off the bridge.

The few seconds of falling are still blurry to me. The fall didn't kill me, but I didn't wake up for quite a while. I suffered a severe blow to the head upon impact. EMTs showed up very soon after I'd hit the ground, and I was rushed to the hospital. I suffered a broken leg, bruised ribs, a broken cheekbone, and serious head trauma, but I never felt any of it. I went into a long, dark, dreamless sleep.

While I was asleep, the world went on. My parents and my brother came to the hospital. My two friends from school came a few hours later. Doctors told them what had happened. I was in a coma. They told friends and family that I could come out of it at any time, but also that I could be like that until I died. There was no telling whether I would actually survive.

The next day, a few kids from my class showed up to visit me. They told my parents that they were sorry about everything. They knew that I was bullied in school and online. One girl said she knew it might have been something someone told me online that pushed me over the edge. The next day more kids showed up to express their sympathy and tell my parents that they wanted to be supportive. They all seemed to feel guilty, like they stood by and let me get bullied.

The next week a group of kids showed up to visit me with a card, and one of the boys went by the name ChamomileT000. He'd always picked on me online. He told my parents that he had said cruel things to me, and he said that not a day went by since he found out I tried to kill myself when he didn't feel like a completely awful human being because he knew he contributed to my reasons for doing it. After awhile, another girl—who went by the name BlackHairedQT online—showed up with her friends and brought flowers and a card.

Groups of kids started to come over, sometimes on their own, just to sit in the room with me. After a month, it became something of a ritual for groups to come and hang out in the room where I was unconscious, just for a half hour or so every week. My parents had forgiven the kids who admitted to bullying me, though they weren't sure how I'd feel when I woke up, if I ever did wake up. No one was making them come to visit, though, and they kept coming to show that they wanted me to live.

I opened my eyes one afternoon after a little more than three months of being unconscious. Only my parents were in the room at the time. They cried and hugged me, and I acknowledged them the best I could. My motor and speech skills were affected quite a bit by the coma, but I told my parents in sobbing, broken sentences that I was sorry for having scared them and that I loved them.

Later that evening, kids from my class started to show up, and they immediately told me they were sorry when they came into the room. My parents told me that the kids had been coming over on a regular basis to be with me and show their support. They had told my parents everything about the bullying, and they all seemed to share in the consensus that they didn't want things like that to happen anymore.

I felt a little pitied at first, like it was put on for me. But a group of girls visited me the day after and wanted to tell me personally that they were sorry for the texts they had sent me the night of the dance, when they were so mean to me. They said they were sorry for acting like bitches, and they told me things would be different from now on in school. They seemed genuine enough. They seemed to want to treat me better. I knew it was probably hard for some of those girls to say they were wrong or to treat me like I was on the same level as they were. But they were being nice to me, for the time being anyway.

I felt a little embarrassed about what I had done, even though no one even once made me feel badly about it. Everyone only told me that they loved me or that they were sorry and wanted me to feel like I belonged.

When the day came for me to go home from the hospital, something happened that helped me believe I was accepted. I came into the house, went to my room, and checked my phone. I had 328 messages accumulated from the three months I was in a coma. When I went through them, none of them were mocking. On the day after I jumped, all of the messages—from everyone, friend and bully—were positive and sent wishes that I would live through it and come out of the coma. The messages became apologies, some of them long and rambling. There were a bunch of "Where are you?" messages from friends who didn't live near me. The rest were messages of "Get better soon" and "We are praying for you to live" and "My friends and I are supporting you and we want you to live."

It became obvious to me that people cared about me who had the same interests as I did and whose lives would be changed if I was not there. I knew that some of the messages were from kids who wanted to band together and send me texts so that I would know, if or when I came out of the coma, that I was not hated by others and that everyone was thinking about me when I wasn't there.They had sent texts over and over, like they were checking on me; it was truly thoughtful.

It was only after I had seen all of the new texts on my phone that I decided I did appreciate my life and that I did want to live. I cried. Knowing that everyone was willing to accept me made me feel a certain happiness—the type of happiness you have when you receive a gift from a person you love. I felt that way when my mother gave me the charm I wear around my neck. I felt confident that I would be able to go forward in my life again and that it wouldn't be all loneliness and sadness. I felt like my life did have meaning and that there would always be friends who cared about me. I have a new hope, too, that someday I will experience that same special happiness when I meet a person who will love me for exactly who I am and think I am beautiful exactly the way I am.

CHAPTER FIFTEEN

IT'S NEVER TOO LATE

It takes one person to forgive; it takes two people to be reunited.

—Lewis B. Smedes

I watched the sun shine over the rolling hills that were home to line after line of gravestones from years past. Everyone in the car was quiet. I was only about seven years old at the time, and I just assumed people were supposed to be quiet during a funeral. I probably would not have understood all of the reasons some people in my family didn't talk to other members. My parents never would let me hear them say something negative or insulting about any of my sisters, aunts, uncles, cousins, or anyone. They were always polite and proper. But all of my relatives were there that day, in the cars in front and behind me.

I would have been more sad, I suppose, if I knew my grandfather that well. He was uncommunicative for the latter part of his life, due to complications from his stint in the army during World War II.

The day of the funeral was the first day I ever saw my father cry. It was unsettling in a way that I had not experienced before, and I didn't want to experience again. He was a powerful, confident person, now helpless and broken down in tears over the death of his father.

We got out of the car and congregated by the gravesite. The priest started to say whatever a priest is supposed to say about ashes to ashes. He offered other hopeful words about going to be with God, peppered with morbid images of decay and portrayals of the transitory nature of human life and all of the things we love on this earth. I can't say I had the attention span for it at that age. But I stood there respectfully.

I caught a glimpse of my sister Christine, who had come with her son and daughter and her husband, Glenn. My father hadn't spoken to Glenn for ten years. I didn't know the whole story at the time—it was just another one of those things that went on between adults that I did not question, nor was I allowed to question under the family mores. (My father believed children should be seen and not heard.)

Christine smiled at me—one of those sour smiles that ended in her putting her head down. It was a smile that said, "I'm trying to stay positive, but everything is actually really bad right now."

Before I was born, my sister Christine ran away from home. She and my father didn't get along very well, and my mother, wanting to be a good parent, would always support my father or stay out of the argument. The fact that my mother didn't stick up for her, I think, probably made Christine really angry. It was just normal teenage stuff they fought about, like not letting her wear certain clothes, hang out with certain people, or go certain places. My dad caught her with pot once or twice, but his first instinct was to punish my older brother, Matt, instead of Christine. Christine and Matt were close. Dad punished Matt instead of Christine, I guess, because he assumed Matt brought the pot into the house and had exposed her to it.

But that was one of the last straws for Christine, watching Matt get struck in the face and yelled at for something that she had done herself. One day, she just basically said, "I'm not going to school today. I'm packing my things up, and I'm going to live with my boyfriend, Glenn. Screw you, Dad."

I believe my dad responded with something like, "If you go out that door, you can't ever come back."

She didn't even look over her shoulder when she left. I mean, I didn't see this happen, I wasn't alive yet, but that's what I hear.

Christine did just what she said. She went and lived with Glenn. Glenn was a kind of rough guy. He worked construction. He didn't mince words. He'd tell you what was up if there was something bothering him about you. He and Christine were happy together. Christine might never have regretted moving in with him, I don't know.

Christine and Dad were on talking terms, but she didn't come around the house, and she never introduced Glenn to them. After the birth of their son, Jake, Christine and Glenn started to warm up to my father a bit, but it didn't last. When they were over at the house one night—I was too young to actually remember any of the details on my own—Dad and Glenn got into some spat about whether Glenn had taken Christine away from him or whether Glenn was doing Dad a favor by taking care of his daughter and providing for her. It ended with Dad kicking Glenn out of the house and telling him he was not welcome there anymore. All I personally remember was that it was not pleasant, and there was a lot of shouting involved. I probably wasn't even allowed to know what had happened. My parents never wanted to give me the idea that there was bad blood or hard feelings between family members. We just didn't talk about it. Glenn did not talk to Dad, and Dad did not talk to Glenn.

As we all dutifully said the words of the prayers and incantations together, I saw Dad, Christine, and Glenn, all together, in the same area at the same time. They were calm and solemn. It was strange. I could tell that they were all trying to just focus on the ceremony and not think about being in each others' company.

When you think negatively about a person, you call them stubborn. When you think positively about a person, you call them committed, confident, or full of self-esteem. Both of these men had that quality—stubbornness and/or self-esteem. They both believed they were right in their opinions about each other, and neither would be moved—at least no one would ever expect them to be moved. Dad thought Glenn was a low life. Glenn thought Dad was an ungrateful old bastard. They had somehow reached an angry stalemate, an affirmation of their mutual inability to live in each other's verbal presence. Yet I could see these two men, engaging in the same prayer-like behavior, only about twelve feet from one another.

The priest finally waved his hand and stopped talking. My father wheeled my grandmother up to the casket, and she placed a flower upon it. My father put his hand over his mouth. He placed a flower on the casket and said goodbye to his father. He cried.

I didn't watch. I tried to ignore it. The others paid their last respects and embraced each other. I watched my sister and Glenn, my brother Matt and his girlfriend Janis, my Aunt Marie, my Uncle Bertrand, and my cousins Robert, Jean-Luc, and Claudette, all pay their respects and walk on, staring at the ground or into empty space. There were countless other relatives, sometimes weighed down by the presence of anxious small children. Then there were a few people I'd never seen before and would never see again. Perhaps they were friends. Perhaps they were casual acquaintances who respected my grandfather in some capacity because of his work.

When the last group of mourners had walked on, the casket was lowered into the ground. There came a moment when Glenn and Dad, whether by coincidence or mutual choice, came face-to-face with each other, with the gravesite in their background. I don't know if what happened was spontaneous. I don't know if it was inspired by my grandfather's passing. I don't know if maybe one of them did secretly think they were wrong about the other. Glenn and Dad came face-to-face with one another and looked at each other. They shook hands. The handshake turned into a hug. I could only make out some of the words that they said—they were talking only to one another and didn't want the crowd to hear. But Glenn said to my father that he was sorry for his loss, that he did care about my father, and that he wished they didn't have to be enemies. Dad told him that he did appreciate Glenn for taking care of Christine, and that he was proud of Glenn and Christine in their happy life with their beautiful children—his grandchildren.

Glenn seemed ready to leave it at that, but then my father said something like, "We don't have to be enemies anymore," and they embraced in front of the gravesite. Everyone was already quiet, but by then the entire family had realized that a reconciliation was happening, and they had crowded around Dad and Glenn, trying to hear what they were saying to one another. When they embraced, everyone applauded. It was like a miracle had happened and everyone just watched it. Everyone went from being solemn to being hopeful, perhaps even a little bit celebratory.

When we all got together at the house afterwards, the mood was light and happy. No one cried. My father didn't cry anymore that day. Something tragic had happened, but then something more beautiful had happened. It was almost like the beautiful thing canceled out the tragic thing for a while that day. There was one less confusing, awkward silence between two of my family members from that day forth.

Experiences like this make me wonder: why do we wait until bad things happen to tell each other we care? If there is something that we ought to say or show to one another before the day is done, we should do it right now! If we wait until it's convenient or appropriate, we are truly stubborn—but that is the rut we fall into.

Glenn and my father had a reason to come together on that day, but the rest of us don't need to wait for a reason. If you love or respect a person and believe that a person deserves your acknowledgement, appreciation, or consideration, you must say it, and you must say it as soon as possible! The convenient or appropriate time might be too late. That time, it was my grandfather's funeral, but I know that both Dad and Glenn knew that everyone passes, and that making peace and having forgiveness between them was an endeavor they were obliged to undertake before one of them passed and their true respects went unpaid. This was a happy ending to a funeral. But the happiest part of this story is that you and I now know that we do not have to wait until a funeral happens to make peace and forgive one another.

ACKNOWLEDGEMENTS

Thanks to my friend and colleague Andreas Saint-Laurent, a great writer who helped me shape these stories. He is a funny and sincere man, and it was a sincere pleasure to work with him to create this book. I also want to express my gratitude to Nadine Edwards, a dear friend and a wise lady who lives every day with a second chance in mind.

I also want to thank my kids, Zak and Jake, who have taught me that redemption and hope can be found every day in the eyes of our children. Lastly, thanks go to my beautiful and sexy wife, Zahra, who gave me a second chance to be a better husband and father!

William Umansky
Orlando, Florida
March 2011

ABOUT THE AUTHOR

William D. Umansky, also known as "The Lawman," is a criminal defense and personal injury lawyer who has made it his life's mission to help others have a second chance at life. As the Managing Partner of the **Umansky Law Firm** in Orlando, Florida, William uses his experience to show people who have gone through life-altering ordeals that in the midst of difficulty, there is a way out.

William and his wife Zahra, also a trial lawyer, and their great boys, Zak and Jake, currently reside in the Central Florida area.

He is also the founder of the **Second Chance Foundation of Florida**, a non-profit foundation that raises money and funds for tuition and book scholarships for outstanding underprivileged high school seniors who need a second chance! For more information go to **SecondChanceofFlorida.com.**